Henry James

Henry James OM (15 April 1843 – 28 February 1916) was an American-British author regarded as a key transitional figure between literary realism and literary modernism, and is considered by many to be among the greatest novelists in the English language. He was the son of Henry James Sr. and the brother of renowned philosopher and psychologist William James and diarist Alice James.

He is best known for a number of novels dealing with the social and marital interplay between émigré Americans, English people, and continental Europeans. Examples of such novels include The Portrait of a Lady, The Ambassadors, and The Wings of the Dove. His later works were increasingly experimental. In describing the internal states of mind and social dynamics of his characters, James often made use of a style in which ambiguous or contradictory motives and impressions were overlaid or juxtaposed in the discussion of a character's psyche.(Source: Wikipedia)

Literary works:

Watch and Ward (1871)
Roderick Hudson (1875)
The American (1877)
The Europeans (1878)
Confidence (1879)
Washington Square (1880)
The Portrait of a Lady (1881)
The Bostonians (1886)
The Princess Casamassima (1886)
The Reverberator (1888)
The Tragic Muse (1890)
The Other House (1896)
The Spoils of Poynton (1897)
What Maisie Knew (1897)
The Awkward Age (1899)
The Sacred Fount (1901)

THE
SELECTED
WORKS
OF
HENRY JAMES
VOL. 23 (OF 36)

GLASSES
GREVILLE FANE

PAPER
SKY
CLASSICS

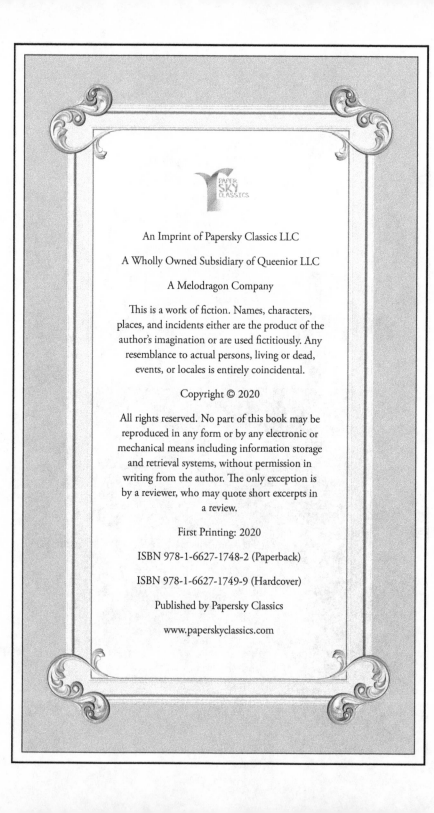

An Imprint of Papersky Classics LLC

A Wholly Owned Subsidiary of Queenior LLC

A Melodragon Company

First Printing: 2020

ISBN 978-1-6627-1748-2 (Paperback)

ISBN 978-1-6627-1749-9 (Hardcover)

Published by Papersky Classics

www.paperskyclassics.com

Contents

THE
SELECTED
WORKS
OF
HENRY JAMES
VOL. 23 (OF 36)

GLASSES

CHAPTER I

Yes indeed, I say to myself, pen in hand, I can keep hold of the thread and let it lead me back to the first impression. The little story is all there, I can touch it from point to point; for the thread, as I call it, is a row of coloured beads on a string. None of the beads are missing—at least I think they're not: that's exactly what I shall amuse myself with finding out.

I had been all summer working hard in town and then had gone down to Folkestone for a blow. Art was long, I felt, and my holiday short; my mother was settled at Folkestone, and I paid her a visit when I could. I remember how on this occasion, after weeks in my stuffy studio with my nose on my palette, I sniffed up the clean salt air and cooled my eyes with the purple sea. The place was full of lodgings, and the lodgings were at that season full of people, people who had nothing to do but to stare at one another on the great flat down. There were thousands of little chairs and almost as many little Jews; and there was music in an open rotunda, over which the little Jews wagged their big noses. We all strolled to and fro and took pennyworths of rest; the long, level cliff-top, edged in places with its iron rail, might have been the deck of a huge crowded ship. There were old folks in Bath chairs, and there was one dear chair, creeping to its last full stop, by the side of which I always walked. There was in fine weather the coast of France to look at, and there were the usual things to say about it; there was also in every state of the atmosphere our friend Mrs. Meldrum, a subject of remark not less inveterate. The widow of an officer in the Engineers, she had settled, like many members of the martial miscellany, well within sight of the hereditary enemy, who however had left her leisure to form in spite of the difference of their years a close alliance with my mother. She was the heartiest, the keenest, the ugliest of women, the least apologetic, the least morbid in her misfortune. She carried it high aloft with loud sounds and free gestures, made it flutter in the breeze as if it had been the flag of her country. It consisted mainly of a big red face, indescribably out of drawing, from which she glared at you through gold-rimmed aids to vision, optic circles of such diameter and so frequently displaced that some one had vividly spoken of her as flattering her nose against the glass of her spectacles. She was extraordinarily near-sighted, and whatever they did to other objects they magnified immensely the kind eyes behind them. Blest conveniences they were, in their hideous, honest strength—they showed the good lady everything in the world but her own queerness. This element was enhanced by wild braveries of dress, reckless charges of colour and stubborn resistances of cut, wondrous encounters in which the art of the toilet seemed to lay down its life. She had the tread of a grenadier and the voice of an angel.

In the course of a walk with her the day after my arrival I found myself grabbing her arm with sudden and undue familiarity. I had been struck by the beauty of a face that approached us and I was still more affected when I saw the face, at the sight of my companion, open like a window thrown wide. A smile fluttered out of it an brightly as a drapery dropped from a sill—a drapery shaken there in the sun by a young lady flanked by two young men, a wonderful young lady who, as we drew nearer, rushed up to Mrs. Meldrum with arms flourished for an embrace. My immediate impression of her had been that she was dressed in mourning, but during the few moments she stood talking with our friend I made more discoveries. The figure from the neck down was meagre, the stature insignificant, but the desire to please towered high, as well as the air of infallibly knowing how and of never, never missing it. This was a little person whom I would have made a high bid for a good chance to paint. The head, the features, the colour, the whole facial oval and radiance had a wonderful purity; the deep grey eyes—the most agreeable, I thought, that I had ever seen—brushed with a kind of winglike grace every object they encountered. Their possessor was just back from Boulogne, where she had spent a week with dear Mrs. Floyd-Taylor: this accounted for the effusiveness of her reunion with dear Mrs. Meldrum. Her black garments were of the freshest and daintiest; she suggested a pink-and-white wreath at a showy funeral. She confounded us for three minutes with her presence; she was a beauty of the great conscious public responsible order. The young men, her companions, gazed at her and grinned: I could see there were very few moments of the day at which young men, these or others, would not be so occupied. The people who approached took leave of their manners; every one seemed to linger and gape. When she brought her face close to Mrs. Meldrum's—and she appeared to be always bringing it close to somebody's—it was a marvel that objects so dissimilar should express the same general identity, the unmistakable character of the English gentlewoman. Mrs. Meldrum sustained the comparison with her usual courage, but I wondered why she didn't introduce me: I should have had no objection to the bringing of such a face close to mine. However, by the time the young lady moved on with her escort she herself bequeathed me a sense that some such *rapprochement* might still occur. Was this by reason of the general frequency of encounters at Folkestone, or by reason of a subtle acknowledgment that she contrived to make of the rights, on the part of others, that such beauty as hers created? I was in a position to answer that question after Mrs. Meldrum had answered a few of mine.

CHAPTER II

Flora Saunt, the only daughter of an old soldier, had lost both her parents, her mother within a few months. Mrs. Meldrum had known them, disapproved of them, considerably avoided them: she had watched the girl, off and on, from her early childhood. Flora, just twenty, was extraordinarily alone in the world—so alone that she had no natural chaperon, no one to stay with but a mercenary stranger, Mrs. Hammond Synge, the sister-in-law of one of the young men I had just seen. She had lots of friends, but none of them nice: she kept picking up impossible people. The Floyd-Taylors, with whom she had been at Boulogne, were simply horrid. The Hammond Synges were perhaps not so vulgar, but they had no conscience in their dealings with her.

"She knows what I think of them," said Mrs. Meldrum, "and indeed she knows what I think of most things."

"She shares that privilege with most of your friends!" I replied laughing.

"No doubt; but possibly to some of my friends it makes a little difference. That girl doesn't care a button. She knows best of all what I think of Flora Saunt."

"And what may your opinion be?"

"Why, that she's not worth troubling about—an idiot too abysmal."

"Doesn't she care for that?"

"Just enough, as you saw, to hug me till I cry out. She's too pleased with herself for anything else to matter."

"Surely, my dear friend," I rejoined, "she has a good deal to be pleased with!"

"So every one tells her, and so you would have told her if I had given you the chance. However, that doesn't signify either, for her vanity is beyond all making or mending. She believes in herself, and she's welcome, after all, poor dear, having only herself to look to. I've seldom met a young woman more completely free to be silly. She has a clear course—she'll make a showy finish."

"Well," I replied, "as she probably will reduce many persons to the same degraded state, her partaking of it won't stand out so much."

"If you mean that the world's full of twaddlers I quite agree with you!" cried Mrs. Meldrum, trumpeting her laugh half across the Channel.

I had after this to consider a little what she would call my mother's son, but I didn't let it prevent me from insisting on her making me acquainted with Flora Saunt; indeed I took the bull by the horns, urging that she had drawn the portrait of a nature which common charity now demanded of her to put into relation with a character really fine. Such a frail creature was just an object of pity. This contention on my part had at first of course been jocular; but strange to say it was quite the ground I found myself taking with regard to our young lady after I had begun to know her. I couldn't have said what I felt about her except that she was undefended; from the first of my sitting with her there after dinner, under the stars—that was a week at Folkestone of balmy nights and muffled tides and crowded chairs—I became aware both that protection was wholly absent from her life and that she was wholly indifferent to its absence. The odd thing was that she was not appealing: she was abjectly, divinely conceited, absurdly fantastically pleased. Her beauty was as yet all the world to her, a world she had plenty to do to live in. Mrs. Meldrum told me more about her, and there was nothing that, as the centre of a group of giggling, nudging spectators, Flora wasn't ready to tell about herself. She held her little court in the crowd, upon the grass, playing her light over Jews and Gentiles, completely at ease in all promiscuities. It was an effect of these things that from the very first, with every one listening, I could mention that my main business with her would be just to have a go at her head and to arrange in that view for an early sitting. It would have been as impossible, I think, to be impertinent to her as it would have been to throw a stone at a plate-glass window; so any talk that went forward on the basis of her loveliness was the most natural thing in the world and immediately became the most general and sociable. It was when I saw all this that I judged how, though it was the last thing she asked for, what one would ever most have at her service was a curious compassion. That sentiment was coloured by the vision of the dire exposure of a being whom vanity had put so off her guard. Hers was the only vanity I have ever known that made its possessor superlatively soft. Mrs. Meldrum's further information contributed moreover to these indulgences—her account of the girl's neglected childhood and queer continental relegations, with straying squabbling Monte-Carlo-haunting parents; the more invidious picture, above all, of her pecuniary arrangement, still in force, with the Hammond Synges, who really, though they never took her out—practically she went out alone—had their hands half the time in her pocket. She had to pay for everything, down to her share of the wine-bills and the horses' fodder, down to Bertie Hammond Synge's fare in the "underground" when he went to the City for her. She had been left with just money enough to turn her head; and it hadn't even been put in trust, nothing prudent or proper had been done with it. She could spend her capital, and at the rate she was going, expensive, extravagant and with a swarm of parasites to help, it certainly wouldn't last very long.

"Couldn't *you* perhaps take her, independent, unencumbered as you are?" I asked of Mrs. Meldrum. "You're probably, with one exception, the sanest person she knows, and you at least wouldn't scandalously fleece her."

"How do you know what I wouldn't do?" my humorous friend demanded. "Of course I've thought how I can help her—it has kept me awake at night. But doing it's impossible; she'll take nothing from me. You know what she does—she hugs me and runs away. She has an instinct about me and feels that I've one about her. And then she dislikes me for another reason that I'm not quite clear about, but that I'm well aware of and that I shall find out some day. So far as her settling with me goes it would be impossible moreover here; she wants naturally enough a much wider field. She must live in London—her game is there. So she takes the line of adoring me, of saying she can never forget that I was devoted to her mother—which I wouldn't for the world have been—and of giving me a wide berth. I think she positively dislikes to look at me. It's all right; there's no obligation; though people in general can't take their eyes off me."

"I see that at this moment," I replied. "But what does it matter where or how, for the present, she lives? She'll marry infallibly, marry early, and everything then will change."

"Whom will she marry?" my companion gloomily asked.

"Any one she likes. She's so abnormally pretty that she can do anything. She'll fascinate some nabob or some prince."

"She'll fascinate him first and bore him afterwards. Moreover she's not so pretty as you make her out; she hasn't a scrap of a figure."

"No doubt, but one doesn't in the least miss it."

"Not now," said Mrs. Meldrum, "but one will when she's older and when everything will have to count."

"When she's older she'll count as a princess, so it won't matter."

"She has other drawbacks," my companion went on. "Those wonderful eyes are good for nothing but to roll about like sugar-balls—which they greatly resemble—in a child's mouth. She can't use them."

"Use them? Why, she does nothing else."

"To make fools of young men, but not to read or write, not to do any sort of work. She never opens a book, and her maid writes her notes. You'll say that those who live in glass houses shouldn't throw stones. Of course I know that if I didn't wear my goggles I shouldn't be good for much."

"Do you mean that Miss Saunt ought to sport such things?" I exclaimed with more horror than I meant to show.

"I don't prescribe for her; I don't know that they're what she requires."

"What's the matter with her eyes?" I asked after a moment.

"I don't exactly know; but I heard from her mother years ago that even as a child they had had for a while to put her into spectacles and that though she hated them and had been in a fury of disgust, she would always have to be extremely careful. I'm sure I hope she is!"

I echoed the hope, but I remember well the impression this made upon me—my immediate pang of resentment, a disgust almost equal to Flora's own. I felt as if a great rare sapphire had split in my hand.

CHAPTER III

This conversation occurred the night before I went back to town. I settled on the morrow to take a late train, so that I had still my morning to spend at Folkestone, where during the greater part of it I was out with my mother. Every one in the place was as usual out with some one else, and even had I been free to go and take leave of her I should have been sure that Flora Saunt would not be at home. Just where she was I presently discovered: she was at the far end of the cliff, the point at which it overhangs the pretty view of Sandgate and Hythe. Her back, however, was turned to this attraction; it rested with the aid of her elbows, thrust slightly behind her so that her scanty little shoulders were raised toward her ears, on the high rail that inclosed the down. Two gentlemen stood before her whose faces we couldn't see but who even as observed from the rear were visibly absorbed in the charming figure-piece submitted to them. I was freshly struck with the fact that this meagre and defective little person, with the cock of her hat and the flutter of her crape, with her eternal idleness, her eternal happiness, her absence of moods and mysteries and the pretty presentation of her feet, which especially now in the supported slope of her posture occupied with their imperceptibility so much of the foreground—I was reminded anew, I say, how our young lady dazzled by some art that the enumeration of her merits didn't explain and that the mention of her lapses didn't affect. Where she was amiss nothing counted, and where she was right everything did. I say she was wanting in mystery, but that after all was her secret. This happened to be my first chance of introducing her to my mother, who had not much left in life but the quiet look from under the hood of her chair at the things which, when she should have quitted those she loved, she could still trust to make the world good for them. I wondered an instant how much she might be moved to trust Flora Saunt, and then while the chair stood still and she waited I went over and asked the girl to come and speak to her. In this way I saw that if one of Flora's attendants was the inevitable young Hammond Synge, master of ceremonies of her regular court, always offering the use of a telescope and accepting that of a cigar, the other was a personage I had not yet encountered, a small pale youth in showy knickerbockers, whose eyebrows and nose and the glued points of whose little moustache were extraordinarily uplifted and sustained. I remember taking him at first for a foreigner and for something of a pretender: I scarce know why unless because of the motive I felt in the stare he fixed on me when I asked Miss Saunt to come away. He struck me a little as a young man practising the social art of impertinence; but it didn't matter, for Flora came away with alacrity, bringing all her prettiness and pleasure and gliding over the grass in that rustle of delicate mourning which made the endless variety of her garments, as a painter could take heed, strike one always as the same obscure elegance. She seated herself on the floor of my mother's chair, a little too much on her right instep as I afterwards gathered, caressing her still hand, smiling up into her cold face, commending and approving her without a reserve and without a doubt. She told her immediately, as if it were something for her to hold on by, that she was soon to sit to me for a "likeness," and these words gave me a chance to enquire if it would be the fate of the picture, should I finish it, to be presented to the young man in the knickerbockers. Her lips, at this, parted in a stare; her eyes darkened to the purple of one of the shadow-patches on the sea. She showed for the passing instant the face of some splendid tragic mask, and I remembered for the inconsequence of it what Mrs. Meldrum had said about her sight. I had derived from this lady a worrying impulse to catechise her, but that didn't seem exactly kind; so I substituted another question, inquiring who the pretty young man in knickerbockers might happen to be.

"Oh a gentleman I met at Boulogne. He has come over to see me." After a moment she added: "Lord Iffield."

I had never heard of Lord Iffield, but her mention of his having been at Boulogne helped me to give him a niche. Mrs. Meldrum had incidentally thrown a certain light on the manners of Mrs. Floyd-Taylor, Flora's recent hostess in that charming town, a lady who, it appeared, had a special vocation for helping rich young men to find a use for their leisure. She had always one or other in hand and had apparently on this occasion pointed her lesson at the rare creature on the opposite coast. I had a vague idea that Boulogne was not a resort of the world's envied; at the same time there might very well have been a strong attraction there even for one of the darlings of fortune. I could perfectly understand in any case that such a darling should be drawn to Folkestone by Flora Saunt. But it was not in truth of these things I was thinking; what was uppermost in my mind was a matter which, though it had no sort of keeping, insisted just then on coming out.

"Is it true, Miss Saunt," I suddenly demanded, "that you're so unfortunate as to have had some warning about your beautiful eyes?"

I was startled by the effect of my words; the girl threw back her head, changing colour from brow to chin. "True? Who in the world says so?" I repented of my question in a flash; the way she met it made it seem cruel, and I felt my mother look at me in some surprise. I took care, in answer to Flora's challenge, not to incriminate Mrs. Meldrum. I answered that the rumour had reached me only in the vaguest form and that if I had been moved to put it to the test my very real interest in her must be held responsible. Her blush died away, but a pair of still prettier tears glistened in its track. "If you ever hear such a thing said again you can say it's a horrid lie!" I had brought on a commotion deeper than any I was prepared for; but it was explained in some degree by the next words she uttered: "I'm happy to say there's nothing the matter with any part of me whatever, not the least little thing!" She spoke with her habitual complacency, with triumphant assurance; she smiled again, and I could see how she wished that she hadn't so taken me up. She turned it off with a laugh. "I've good eyes, good teeth, a good digestion and a good temper. I'm sound of wind and limb!" Nothing could have been more characteristic than her blush and her tears, nothing less acceptable to her than to be thought not perfect in every particular. She couldn't submit to the imputation of a flaw. I expressed my delight in what she told me, assuring her I should always do battle for her; and as if to rejoin her companions she got up from her place on my mother's toes. The young men presented their backs to us; they were leaning on the rail of the cliff. Our incident had produced a certain awkwardness, and while I was thinking of what next to say she exclaimed irrelevantly: "Don't you know? He'll be Lord Considine." At that moment the youth marked for this high destiny turned round, and she spoke to my mother. "I'll introduce him to you—he's awfully nice." She beckoned and invited him with her parasol; the movement struck me as taking everything for granted. I had heard of Lord Considine and if I had not been able to place Lord Iffield it was because I didn't know the name of his eldest son. The young man took no notice of Miss Saunt's appeal; he only stared a moment and then on her repeating it quietly turned his back. She was an odd creature: she didn't blush at this; she only said to my mother apologetically, but with the frankest sweetest amusement, "You don't mind, do you? He's a monster of shyness!" It was as if she were sorry for every one—for Lord Iffield, the victim of a complaint so painful, and for my mother, the subject of a certain slight. "I'm sure I don't want him!" said my mother, but Flora added some promise of how she would handle him for his rudeness. She would clearly never explain anything by any failure of her own appeal. There rolled over me while she took leave of us and floated back to her friends a wave of superstitious dread. I seemed somehow to see her go forth to her fate, and yet what should fill out this orb of a high destiny if not such beauty and such joy? I had a dim idea that Lord Considine was a great proprietor, and though there mingled with it a faint impression that I shouldn't like his son the result of the two images was a whimsical prayer that the girl mightn't miss her possible fortune.

CHAPTER IV

One day in the course of the following June there was ushered into my studio a gentleman whom I had not yet seen but with whom I had been very briefly in correspondence. A letter from him had expressed to me some days before his regret on learning that my "splendid portrait" of Miss Flora Louisa Saunt, whose full name figured by her own wish in the catalogue of the exhibition of the Academy, had found a purchaser before the close of the private view. He took the liberty of inquiring whether I might have at his service some other memorial of the same lovely head, some preliminary sketch, some study for the picture. I had replied that I had indeed painted Miss Saunt more than once and that if he were interested in my work I should be happy to show him what I had done. Mr. Geoffrey Dawling, the person thus introduced to me, stumbled into my room with awkward movements and equivocal sounds—a long, lean, confused, confusing young man, with a bad complexion and large protrusive teeth. He bore in its most indelible pressure the postmark, as it were, of Oxford, and as soon as he opened his mouth I perceived, in addition to a remarkable revelation of gums, that the text of the queer communication matched the registered envelope. He was full of refinements and angles, of dreary and distinguished knowledge. Of his unconscious drollery his dress freely partook; it seemed, from the gold ring into which his red necktie was passed to the square toe-caps of his boots, to conform with a high sense of modernness to the fashion before the last. There were moments when his overdone urbanity, all suggestive stammers and interrogative quavers, made him scarcely intelligible; but I felt him to be a gentleman and I liked the honesty of his errand and the expression of his good green eyes.

As a worshipper at the shrine of beauty, however, he needed explaining, especially when I found he had no acquaintance with my brilliant model; had on the mere evidence of my picture taken, as he said, a tremendous fancy to her looks. I ought doubtless to have been humiliated by the simplicity of his judgment of them, a judgment for which the rendering was lost in the subject, quite leaving out the element of art. He was like the innocent reader for whom the story is "really true" and the author a negligible quantity. He had come to me only because he wanted to purchase, and I remember being so amused at his attitude, which I had never seen equally marked in a person of education, that I asked him why, for the sort of enjoyment he desired, it wouldn't be more to the point to deal directly with the lady. He stared and blushed at this; the idea clearly alarmed him. He was an extraordinary case—personally so modest that I could see it had never occurred to him. He had fallen in love with a painted sign and seemed content just to dream of what it stood for. He was the young prince in the legend or the comedy who loses his heart to the miniature of the princess beyond seas. Until I knew him better this puzzled me much—the link was so missing between his sensibility and his type. He was of course bewildered by my sketches, which implied in the beholder some sense of intention and quality; but for one of them, a comparative failure, he ended by conceiving a preference so arbitrary and so lively that, taking no second look at the others, he expressed his wish to possess it and fell into the extremity of confusion over the question of price. I helped him over that stile, and he went off without having asked me a direct question about Miss Saunt, yet with his acquisition under his arm. His delicacy was such that he evidently considered his rights to be limited; he had acquired none at all in regard to the original of the picture. There were others—for I was curious about him—that I wanted him to feel I conceded: I should have been glad of his carrying away a sense of ground acquired for coming back. To ensure this I had probably only to invite him, and I perfectly recall the impulse that made me forbear. It operated suddenly from within while he hung about the door and in spite of the diffident appeal that blinked in his gentle grin. If he was smitten with Flora's ghost what mightn't be the direct force of the luminary that could cast such a shadow? This source of radiance, flooding my poor place, might very well happen to be present the next time he should turn up. The idea was sharp within me that there were relations and complications it was no mission of mine to bring about. If they were to develop they should develop in their very own sense.

Let me say at once that they did develop and that I perhaps after all had something to do with it. If Mr. Dawling had departed without a fresh appointment he was to reappear six months later under protection no less powerful than that of our young lady herself. I had seen her repeatedly for months: she had grown to regard my studio as the temple of her beauty. This miracle was recorded and celebrated there as nowhere else; in other places there was occasional reference to other subjects of remark. The degree of her presumption continued to be stupefying; there was nothing so extraordinary save the degree in which she never paid for it. She was kept innocent, that is she was kept safe, by her egotism, but she was helped also, though she had now put off her mourning, by the attitude of the lone orphan who had to be a law unto herself. It was as a lone orphan that she came and went, as a lone orphan that she was the centre of a crush. The neglect of the Hammond Synges gave relief to this character, and she made it worth their while to be, as every one said, too shocking. Lord Iffield had gone to India to shoot tigers, but he returned in time for the punctual private view: it was he who had snapped up, as Flora called it, the gem of the exhibition. My hope for the girl's future had slipped ignominiously off his back, but after his purchase of the portrait I tried to cultivate a new faith. The girl's own faith was wonderful. It couldn't however be contagious: too great was the limit of her sense of what painters call values. Her colours were laid on like blankets on a cold night. How indeed could a person speak the truth who was always posturing and bragging? She was after all vulgar enough, and by the time I had mastered her profile and could almost with my eyes shut do it in a single line I was decidedly tired of its "purity," which affected me at last as inane. One moved with her, moreover, among phenomena mismated and unrelated; nothing in her talk ever matched anything out of it. Lord Iffield was dying of love for her, but his family was leading him a life. His mother, horrid woman, had told some one that she would rather he should be swallowed by a tiger than marry a girl not absolutely one of themselves. He had given his young friend unmistakable signs, but was lying low, gaining time: it was in his father's power to be, both in personal and in pecuniary ways, excessively nasty to him. His father wouldn't last for ever—quite the contrary; and he knew how thoroughly, in spite of her youth, her beauty and the swarm of her admirers, some of them positively threatening in their passion, he could trust her to hold out. There were richer, cleverer men, there were greater personages too, but she liked her "little viscount" just as he was, and liked to think that, bullied and persecuted, he had her there so gratefully to rest upon. She came back to me with tale upon tale, and it all might be or mightn't. I never met my pretty model in the world—she moved, it appeared, in exalted circles—and could only admire, in her wealth of illustration, the grandeur of her life and the freedom of her hand.

I had on the first opportunity spoken to her of Geoffrey Dawling, and she had listened to my story so far as she had the art of such patience, asking me indeed more questions about him than I could answer; then she had capped my anecdote with others much more striking, the disclosure of effects produced in the most extraordinary quarters: on people who had followed her into railway carriages; guards and porters even who had literally stuck there; others who had spoken to her in shops and hung about her house door; cabmen, upon her honour, in London, who, to gaze their fill at her, had found excuses to thrust their petrifaction through the very glasses of four-wheelers. She lost herself in these reminiscences, the moral of which was that poor Mr. Dawling was only one of a million. When therefore the next autumn she flourished into my studio with her odd companion at her heels her first care was to make clear to me that if he was now in servitude it wasn't because she had run after him. Dawling explained with a hundred grins that when one wished very much to get anything one usually ended by doing so—a proposition which led me wholly to dissent and our young lady to asseverate that she hadn't in the least wished to get Mr. Dawling. She mightn't have wished to get him, but she wished to show him, and I seemed to read that if she could treat him as a trophy her affairs were rather at the ebb. True there always hung from her belt a promiscuous fringe of scalps. Much at any rate would have come and gone since our separation in July. She had spent four months abroad, where, on Swiss and Italian lakes, in German cities, in the French capital, many accidents might have happened.

CHAPTER V

I had been again with my mother, but except Mrs. Meldrum and the gleam of France had not found at Folkestone my old resources and pastimes. Mrs. Meldrum, much edified by my report of the performances, as she called them, in my studio, had told me that to her knowledge Flora would soon be on the straw: she had cut from her capital such fine fat slices that there was almost nothing more left to swallow. Perched on her breezy cliff the good lady dazzled me as usual by her universal light: she knew so much more about everything and everybody than I could ever squeeze out of my colour-tubes. She knew that Flora was acting on system and absolutely declined to be interfered with: her precious reasoning was that her money would last as long as she should need it, that a magnificent marriage would crown her charms before she should be really pinched. She had a sum put by for a liberal outfit; meanwhile the proper use of the rest was to decorate her for the approaches to the altar, keep her afloat in the society in which she would most naturally meet her match. Lord Iffield had been seen with her at Lucerne, at Cadenabbia; but it was Mrs. Meldrum's conviction that nothing was to be expected of him but the most futile flirtation. The girl had a certain hold of him, but with a great deal of swagger he hadn't the spirit of a sheep: he was in fear of his father and would never commit himself in Lord Considine's lifetime. The most Flora might achieve was that he wouldn't marry some one else. Geoffrey Dawling, to Mrs. Meldrum's knowledge (I had told her of the young man's visit) had attached himself on the way back from Italy to the Hammond Synge group. My informant was in a position to be definite about this dangler; she knew about his people; she had heard of him before. Hadn't he been a friend of one of her nephews at Oxford? Hadn't he spent the Christmas holidays precisely three years before at her brother-in-law's in Yorkshire, taking that occasion to get himself refused with derision by wilful Betty, the second daughter of the house? Her sister, who liked the floundering youth, had written to her to complain of Betty, and that the young man should now turn up as an appendage of Flora's was one of those oft-cited proofs that the world is small and that there are not enough people to go round. His father had been something or other in the Treasury; his grandfather on the mother's side had been something or other in the Church. He had come into the paternal estate, two or three thousand a year in Hampshire; but he had let the place advantageously and was generous to four plain sisters who lived at Bournemouth and adored him. The family was hideous all round, but the very salt of the earth. He was supposed to be unspeakably clever; he was fond of London, fond of books, of intellectual society and of the idea of a political career. That such a man should be at the same time fond of Flora Saunt attested, as the phrase in the first volume of Gibbon has it, the variety of his inclinations. I was soon to learn that he was fonder of her than of all the other things together. Betty, one of five and with views above her station, was at any rate felt at home to have dished herself by her perversity. Of course no one had looked at her since and no one would ever look at her again. It would be eminently desirable that Flora should learn the lesson of Betty's fate.

I was not struck, I confess, with all this in my mind, by any symptom on our young lady's part of that sort of meditation. The one moral she saw in anything was that of her incomparable aspect, which Mr. Dawling, smitten even like the railway porters and the cabmen by the doom-dealing gods, had followed from London to Venice and from Venice back to London again. I afterwards learned that her version of this episode was profusely inexact: his personal acquaintance with her had been determined by an accident remarkable enough, I admit, in connexion with what had gone before—a coincidence at all events superficially striking. At Munich, returning from a tour in the Tyrol with two of his sisters, he had found himself at the table d'hôte of his inn opposite to the full presentment of that face of which the mere clumsy copy had made him dream and desire. He had been tossed by it to a height so vertiginous as to involve a retreat from the board; but the next day he had dropped with a resounding thud at the very feet of his apparition. On the following, with an equal incoherence, a sacrifice even of his bewildered sisters, whom he left behind, he made an heroic effort to escape by flight from a fate of which he had already felt the cold breath. That fate, in London, very little later, drove him straight before it—drove him one Sunday afternoon, in the rain, to the door of the Hammond Synges. He marched in other words close up to the cannon that was to blow him to pieces. But three weeks, when he reappeared to me, had elapsed since then, yet (to vary my metaphor) the burden he was to carry for the rest of his days was firmly lashed to his back. I don't mean by this that Flora had been persuaded to contract her scope; I mean that he had been treated to the unconditional snub which, as the event was to show, couldn't have been bettered as a means of securing him. She hadn't calculated, but she had said "Never!" and that word had made a bed big enough for his long-legged patience. He became from this moment to my mind the interesting figure in the piece.

Now that he had acted without my aid I was free to show him this, and having on his own side something to show me he repeatedly knocked at my door. What he brought with him on these occasions was a simplicity so huge that, as I turn my ear to the past, I seem even now to hear it bumping up and down my stairs. That was really what I saw of him in the light of his behaviour. He had fallen in love as he might have broken his leg, and the fracture was of a sort that would make him permanently lame. It was the whole man who limped and lurched, with nothing of him left in the same position as before. The tremendous cleverness, the literary society, the political ambition, the Bournemouth sisters all seemed to flop with his every movement a little nearer to the floor. I hadn't had an Oxford training and I had never encountered the great man at whose feet poor Dawling had most submissively sat and who had addressed him his most destructive sniffs; but I remember asking myself how effectively this privilege had supposed itself to prepare him for the career on which my friend appeared now to have embarked. I remember too making up my mind about the cleverness, which had its uses and I suppose in impenetrable shades even its critics, but from which the friction of mere personal intercourse was not the sort of process to extract a revealing spark. He accepted without a question both his fever and his chill, and the only thing he touched with judgment was this convenience of my friendship. He doubtless told me his simple story, but the matter comes back in a kind of sense of my being rather the mouthpiece, of my having had to put it together for him. He took it from me in this form without a groan, and I gave it him quite as it came; he took it again and again, spending his odd half-hours with me as if for the very purpose of learning how idiotically he was in love. He told me I made him see things: to begin with, hadn't I first made him see Flora Saunt? I wanted him to give her up and lucidly informed him why; on which he never protested nor contradicted, never was even so alembicated as to declare just for the sake of the point that he wouldn't. He simply and pointlessly didn't, and when at the end of three months I asked him what was the use of talking with such a fellow his nearest approach to a justification was to say that what made him want to help her was just the deficiencies I dwelt on. I could only reply without gross developments: "Oh if you're as sorry for her as that!" I too was nearly as sorry for her as that, but it only led me to be sorrier still for other victims of this compassion. With Dawling as with me the compassion was at first in excess of any visible motive; so that when eventually the motive was supplied each could to a certain extent compliment the other on the fineness of his foresight.

After he had begun to haunt my studio Miss Saunt quite gave it up, and I finally learned that she accused me of conspiring with him to put pressure on her to marry him. She didn't know I would take it that way, else she would never have brought him to see me. It was in her view a part of the conspiracy that to show him a kindness I asked him at last to sit to me. I dare say moreover she was disgusted to hear that I had ended by attempting almost as many sketches of his beauty as I had attempted of hers. What was the value of tributes to beauty by a hand that could so abase itself? My relation to poor Dawling's want of modelling was simple enough. I was really digging in that sandy desert for the buried treasure of his soul.

CHAPTER VI

It befell at this period, just before Christmas, that on my having gone under pressure of the season into a great shop to buy a toy or two, my eyes fleeing from superfluity, lighted at a distance on the bright concretion of Flora Saunt, an exhibitability that held its own even against the most plausible pinkness of the most developed dolls. A huge quarter of the place, the biggest bazaar "on earth," was peopled with these and other effigies and fantasies, as well as with purchasers and vendors haggard alike, in the blaze of the gas, with hesitations. I was just about to appeal to Flora to avert that stage of my errand when I saw that she was accompanied by a gentleman whose identity, though more than a year had elapsed, came back to me from the Folkestone cliff. It had been associated on that scene with showy knickerbockers; at present it overflowed more splendidly into a fur-trimmed overcoat. Lord Iffield's presence made me waver an instant before crossing over, and during that instant Flora, blank and undistinguishing, as if she too were after all weary of alternatives, looked straight across at me. I was on the point of raising my hat to her when I observed that her face gave no sign. I was exactly in the line of her vision, but she either didn't see me or didn't recognise me, or else had a reason to pretend she didn't. Was her reason that I had displeased her and that she wished to punish me? I had always thought it one of her merits that she wasn't vindictive. She at any rate simply looked away; and at this moment one of the shop-girls, who had apparently gone off in search of it, bustled up to her with a small mechanical toy. It so happened that I followed closely what then took place, afterwards recognising that I had been led to do so, led even through the crowd to press nearer for the purpose, by an impression of which in the act I was not fully conscious.

Flora with the toy in her hand looked round at her companion; then seeing his attention had been solicited in another quarter she moved away with the shop-girl, who had evidently offered to conduct her into the presence of more objects of the same sort. When she reached the indicated spot I was in a position still to observe her. She had asked some question about the working of the toy, and the girl, taking it herself, began to explain the little secret. Flora bent her head over it, but she clearly didn't understand. I saw her, in a manner that quickened my curiosity, give a glance back at the place from which she had come. Lord Iffield was talking with another young person; she satisfied herself of this by the aid of a question addressed to her own attendant. She then drew closer to the table near which she stood and, turning her back to me, bent her head lower over the collection of toys and more particularly over the small object the girl had attempted to explain. She took it again and, after a moment, with her face well averted, made an odd motion of her arms and a significant little duck of her head. These slight signs, singular as it may appear, produced in my bosom an agitation so great that I failed to notice Lord Iffield's whereabouts. He had rejoined her; he was close upon her before I knew it or before she knew it herself. I felt at that instant the strangest of all promptings: if it could have operated more rapidly it would have caused me to dash between them in some such manner as to give Flora a caution. In fact as it was I think I could have done this in time had I not been checked by a curiosity stronger still than my impulse. There were three seconds during which I saw the young man and yet let him come on. Didn't I make the quick calculation that if he didn't catch what Flora was doing I too might perhaps not catch it? She at any rate herself took the alarm. On perceiving her companion's nearness she made, still averted, another duck of her head and a shuffle of her hands so precipitate that a little tin steamboat she had been holding escaped from them and rattled down to the floor with a sharpness that I hear at this hour. Lord Iffield had already seized her arm; with a violent jerk he brought her round toward him. Then it was that there met my eyes a quite distressing sight: this exquisite creature, blushing, glaring, exposed, with a pair of big black-rimmed eye-glasses, defacing her by their position, crookedly astride of her beautiful nose. She made a grab at them with her free hand while I turned confusedly away.

CHAPTER VII

I don't remember how soon it was I spoke to Geoffrey Dawling; his sittings were irregular, but it was certainly the very next time he gave me one.

"Has any rumour ever reached you of Miss Saunt's having anything the matter with her eyes?" He stared with a candour that was a sufficient answer to my question, backing it up with a shocked and mystified "Never!" Then I asked him if he had observed in her any symptom, however disguised, of embarrassed sight; on which, after a moment's thought, he exclaimed "Disguised?" as if my use of that word had vaguely awakened a train. "She's not a bit myopic," he said; "she doesn't blink or contract her lids." I fully recognised this and I mentioned that she altogether denied the impeachment; owing it to him moreover to explain the ground of my inquiry, I gave him a sketch of the incident that had taken place before me at the shop. He knew all about Lord Iffield; that nobleman had figured freely in our conversation as his preferred, his injurious rival. Poor Dawling's contention was that if there had been a definite engagement between his lordship and the young lady, the sort of thing that was announced in the Morning Post, renunciation and retirement would be comparatively easy to him; but that having waited in vain for any such assurance he was entitled to act as if the door were not really closed or were at any rate not cruelly locked. He was naturally much struck with my anecdote and still more with my interpretation of it.

"There *is* something, there *is* something—possibly something very grave, certainly something that requires she should make use of artificial aids. She won't admit it publicly, because with her idolatry of her beauty, the feeling she is all made up of, she sees in such aids nothing but the humiliation and the disfigurement. She has used them in secret, but that is evidently not enough, for the affection she suffers from, apparently some definite menace, has lately grown much worse. She looked straight at me in the shop, which was violently lighted, without seeing it was I. At the same distance, at Folkestone, where as you know I first met her, where I heard this mystery hinted at and where she indignantly denied the thing, she appeared easily enough to recognise people. At present she couldn't really make out anything the shop-girl showed her. She has successfully concealed from the man I saw her with that she resorts in private to a pince-nez and that she does so not only under the strictest orders from her oculist, but because literally the poor thing can't accomplish without such help half the business of life. Iffield however has suspected something, and his suspicions, whether expressed or kept to himself, have put him on the watch. I happened to have a glimpse of the movement at which he pounced on her and caught her in the act."

I had thought it all out; my idea explained many things, and Dawling turned pale as he listened to me.

"Was he rough with her?" he anxiously asked.

"How can I tell what passed between them? I fled from the place."

My companion stared. "Do you mean to say her eyesight's going?"

"Heaven forbid! In that case how could she take life as she does?"

"How *does* she take life? That's the question!" He sat there bewilderedly brooding; the tears rose to his lids; they reminded me of those I had seen in Flora's the day I risked my enquiry. The question he had asked was one that to my own satisfaction I was ready to answer, but I hesitated to let him hear as yet all that my reflections had suggested. I was indeed privately astonished at their ingenuity. For the present I only rejoined that it struck me she was playing a particular game; at which he went on as if he hadn't heard me, suddenly haunted with a fear, lost in the dark possibility. "Do you mean there's a danger of anything very bad?"

"My dear fellow, you must ask her special adviser."

"Who in the world is her special adviser?"

"I haven't a conception. But we mustn't get too excited. My impression would be that she has only to observe a few ordinary rules, to exercise a little common sense."

Dawling jumped at this. "I see—to stick to the pince-nez."

"To follow to the letter her oculist's prescription, whatever it is and at whatever cost to her prettiness. It's not a thing to be trifled with."

"Upon my honour it *shan't* be!" he roundly declared; and he adjusted himself to his position again as if we had quite settled the business. After a considerable interval, while I botched away, he suddenly said: "Did they make a great difference?"

"A great difference?"

"Those things she had put on."

"Oh the glasses—in her beauty? She looked queer of course, but it was partly because one was unaccustomed. There are women who look charming in nippers. What, at any rate, if she does look queer? She must be mad not to accept that alternative."

"She *is* mad," said Geoffrey Dawling.

"Mad to refuse you, I grant. Besides," I went on, "the pince-nez, which was a large and peculiar one, was all awry: she had half pulled it off, but it continued to stick, and she was crimson, she was angry."

"It must have been horrible!" my companion groaned.

"It *was* horrible. But it's still more horrible to defy all warnings; it's still more horrible to be landed in—" Without saying in what I disgustedly shrugged my shoulders.

After a glance at me Dawling jerked round. "Then you do believe that she may be?"

I hesitated. "The thing would be to make *her* believe it. She only needs a good scare."

"But if that fellow is shocked at the precautions she does take?"

"Oh who knows?" I rejoined with small sincerity. "I don't suppose Iffield is absolutely a brute."

"I would take her with leather blinders, like a shying mare!" cried Geoffrey Dawling.

I had an impression that Iffield wouldn't, but I didn't communicate it, for I wanted to pacify my friend, whom I had discomposed too much for the purposes of my sitting. I recollect that I did some good work that morning, but it also comes back to me that before we separated he had practically revealed to me that my anecdote, connecting itself in his mind with a series of observations at the time unconscious and unregistered, had covered with light the subject of our colloquy. He had had a formless perception of some secret that drove Miss Saunt to subterfuges, and the more he thought of it the more he guessed this secret to be the practice of making believe she saw when she didn't and of cleverly keeping people from finding out how little she saw. When one pieced things together it was astonishing what ground they covered. Just as he was going away he asked me from what source at Folkestone the horrid tale had proceeded. When I had given him, as I saw no reason not to do, the name of Mrs. Meldrum he exclaimed: "Oh I know all about her; she's a friend of some friends of mine!" At this I remembered wilful Betty and said to myself that I knew some one who would probably prove more wilful still.

CHAPTER VIII

A few days later I again heard Dawling on my stairs, and even before he passed my threshold I knew he had something to tell.

"I've been down to Folkestone—it was necessary I should see her!" I forget whether he had come straight from the station; he was at any rate out of breath with his news, which it took me however a minute to apply.

"You mean that you've been with Mrs. Meldrum?"

"Yes, to ask her what she knows and how she comes to know it. It worked upon me awfully—I mean what you told me." He made a visible effort to seem quieter than he was, and it showed me sufficiently that he had not been reassured. I laid, to comfort him and smiling at a venture, a friendly hand on his arm, and he dropped into my eyes, fixing them an instant, a strange distended look which might have expressed the cold clearness of all that was to come. "I *know*—now!" he said with an emphasis he rarely used.

"What then did Mrs. Meldrum tell you?"

"Only one thing that signified, for she has no real knowledge. But that one thing was everything."

"What is it then?"

"Why, that she can't bear the sight of her." His pronouns required some arranging, but after I had successfully dealt with them I replied that I was quite aware of Miss Saunt's trick of turning her back on the good lady of Folkestone. Only what did that prove? "Have you never guessed? I guessed as soon as she spoke!" Dawling towered over me in dismal triumph. It was the first time in our acquaintance that, on any ground of understanding this had occurred; but even so remarkable an incident still left me sufficiently at sea to cause him to continue: "Why, the effect of those spectacles!"

I seemed to catch the tail of his idea. "Mrs. Meldrum's?"

"They're so awfully ugly and they add so to the dear woman's ugliness." This remark began to flash a light, and when he quickly added "She sees herself, she sees her own fate!" my response was so immediate that I had almost taken the words out of his mouth. While I tried to fix this sudden image of Flora's face glazed in and cross-barred even as Mrs. Meldrum's was glazed and barred, he went on to assert that only the horror of that image, looming out at herself, could be the reason of her avoiding the person who so forced it home. The fact he had encountered made everything hideously vivid, and more vivid than anything else that just such another pair of goggles was what would have been prescribed to Flora.

"I see—I see," I presently returned. "What would become of Lord Iffield if she were suddenly to come out in them? What indeed would become of every one, what would become of everything?" This was an enquiry that Dawling was evidently unprepared to meet, and I completed it by saying at last: "My dear fellow, for that matter, what would become of *you?*"

Once more he turned on me his good green eyes. "Oh I shouldn't mind!"

The tone of his words somehow made his ugly face beautiful, and I discovered at this moment how much I really liked him. None the less, at the same time, perversely and rudely, I felt the droll side of our discussion of such alternatives. It made me laugh out and say to him while I laughed: "You'd take her even with those things of Mrs. Meldrum's?"

He remained mournfully grave; I could see that he was surprised at my rude mirth. But he summoned back a vision of the lady at Folkestone and conscientiously replied: "Even with those things of Mrs. Meldrum's." I begged him not to resent my laughter, which but exposed the fact that we had built a monstrous castle in the air. Didn't he see on what flimsy ground the structure rested? The evidence was preposterously small. He believed the worst, but we were really uninformed.

"I shall find out the truth," he promptly replied.

"How can you? If you question her you'll simply drive her to perjure herself. Wherein after all does it concern you to know the truth? It's the girl's own affair."

"Then why did you tell me your story?"

I was a trifle embarrassed. "To warn you off," I smiled. He took no more notice of these words than presently to remark that Lord Iffield had no serious intentions. "Very possibly," I said. "But you mustn't speak as if Lord Iffield and you were her only alternatives."

Dawling thought a moment. "Couldn't something be got out of the people she has consulted? She must have been to people. How else can she have been condemned?"

"Condemned to what? Condemned to perpetual nippers? Of course she has consulted some of the big specialists, but she has done it, you may be sure, in the most clandestine manner; and even if it were supposable that they would tell you anything—which I altogether doubt—you would have great difficulty in finding out which men they are. Therefore leave it alone; never show her what you suspect."

I even before he quitted me asked him to promise me this. "All right, I promise"—but he was gloomy enough. He was a lover facing the fact that there was no limit to the deceit his loved one was ready to practise: it made so remarkably little difference. I could see by what a stretch his passionate pity would from this moment overlook the girl's fatuity and folly. She was always accessible to him—that I knew; for if she had told him he was an idiot to dream she could dream of him, she would have rebuked the imputation of having failed to make it clear that she would always be glad to regard him as a friend. What were most of her friends—what were all of them—but repudiated idiots? I was perfectly aware that in her conversations and confidences I myself for instance had a niche in the gallery. As regards poor Dawling I knew how often he still called on the Hammond Synges. It was not there but under the wing of the Floyd-Taylors that her intimacy with Lord Iffield most flourished. At all events, when a week after the visit I have just summarised Flora's name was one morning brought up to me, I jumped at the conclusion that Dawling had been with her, and even I fear briefly entertained the thought that he had broken his word.

41

CHAPTER IX

She left me, after she had been introduced, in no suspense about her present motive; she was on the contrary in a visible fever to enlighten me; but I promptly learned that for the alarm with which she pitiably panted our young man was not accountable. She had but one thought in the world, and that thought was for Lord Iffield. I had the strangest saddest scene with her, and if it did me no other good it at least made me at last completely understand why insidiously, from the first, she had struck me as a creature of tragedy. In showing me the whole of her folly it lifted the curtain of her misery. I don't know how much she meant to tell me when she came—I think she had had plans of elaborate misrepresentation; at any rate she found it at the end of ten minutes the simplest way to break down and sob, to be wretched and true. When she had once begun to let herself go the movement took her off her feet; the relief of it was like the cessation of a cramp. She shared in a word her long secret, she shifted her sharp pain. She brought, I confess, tears to my own eyes, tears of helpless tenderness for her helpless poverty. Her visit however was not quite so memorable in itself as in some of its consequences, the most immediate of which was that I went that afternoon to see Geoffrey Dawling, who had in those days rooms in Welbeck Street, where I presented myself at an hour late enough to warrant the supposition that he might have come in. He had not come in, but he was expected, and I was invited to enter and wait for him: a lady, I was informed, was already in his sitting-room. I hesitated, a little at a loss: it had wildly coursed through my brain that the lady was perhaps Flora Saunt. But when I asked if she were young and remarkably pretty I received so significant a "No sir!" that I risked an advance and after a minute in this manner found myself, to my astonishment, face to face with Mrs. Meldrum.

"Oh you dear thing," she exclaimed, "I'm delighted to see you: you spare me another compromising démarche! But for this I should have called on you also. Know the worst at once: if you see me here it's at least deliberate—it's planned, plotted, shameless. I came up on purpose to see him, upon my word I'm in love with him. Why, if you valued my peace of mind, did you let him the other day at Folkestone dawn upon my delighted eyes? I found myself there in half an hour simply infatuated with him. With a perfect sense of everything that can be urged against him I hold him none the less the very pearl of men. However, I haven't come up to declare my passion—I've come to bring him news that will interest him much more. Above all I've come to urge upon him to be careful."

"About Flora Saunt?"

"About what he says and does: he must be as still as a mouse! She's at last really engaged."

"But it's a tremendous secret?" I was moved to mirth.

"Precisely: she wired me this noon, and spent another shilling to tell me that not a creature in the world is yet to know it."

"She had better have spent it to tell you that she had just passed an hour with the creature you see before you."

"She has just passed an hour with every one in the place!" Mrs. Meldrum cried. "They've vital reasons, she says, for it's not coming out for a month. Then it will be formally announced, but meanwhile her rejoicing is wild. I daresay Mr. Dawling already knows and, as it's nearly seven o'clock, may have jumped off London Bridge. But an effect of the talk I had with him the other day was to make me, on receipt of my telegram, feel it to be my duty to warn him in person against taking action, so to call it, on the horrid certitude which I could see he carried away with him. I had added somehow to that certitude. He told me what you had told him you had seen in your shop."

Mrs. Meldrum, I perceived, had come to Welbeck Street on an errand identical with my own—a circumstance indicating her rare sagacity, inasmuch as her ground for undertaking it was a very different thing from what Flora's wonderful visit had made of mine. I remarked to her that what I had seen in the shop was sufficiently striking, but that I had seen a great deal more that morning in my studio. "In short," I said, "I've seen everything."

She was mystified. "Everything?"

"The poor creature is under the darkest of clouds. Oh she came to triumph, but she remained to talk something in the nature of sense! She put herself completely in my hands—she does me the honour to intimate that of all her friends I'm the most disinterested. After she had announced to me that Lord Iffield was utterly committed to her and that for the present I was absolutely the only person in the secret, she arrived at her real business. She had had a suspicion of me ever since that day at Folkestone when I asked her for the truth about her eyes. The truth is what you and I both guessed. She's in very bad danger."

"But from what cause? I, who by God's mercy have kept mine, know everything that can be known about eyes," said Mrs. Meldrum.

"She might have kept hers if she had profited by God's mercy, if she had done in time, done years ago, what was imperatively ordered her; if she hadn't in fine been cursed with the loveliness that was to make her behaviour a thing of fable. She may still keep her sight, or what remains of it, if she'll sacrifice—and after all so little—that purely superficial charm. She must do as you've done; she must wear, dear lady, what you wear!"

What my companion wore glittered for the moment like a melon-frame in August. "Heaven forgive her—now I understand!" She flushed for dismay.

But I wasn't afraid of the effect on her good nature of her thus seeing, through her great goggles, why it had always been that Flora held her at such a distance. "I can't tell you," I said, "from what special affection, what state of the eye, her danger proceeds: that's the one thing she succeeded this morning in keeping from me. She knows it herself perfectly; she has had the best advice in Europe. 'It's a thing that's awful, simply awful'—that was the only account she would give me. Year before last, while she was at Boulogne, she went for three days with Mrs. Floyd-Taylor to Paris. She there surreptitiously consulted the greatest man—even Mrs. Floyd-Taylor doesn't know. Last autumn in Germany she did the same. 'First put on certain special spectacles with a straight bar in the middle: then we'll talk'—that's practically what they say. What *she* says is that she'll put on anything in nature when she's married, but that she must get married first. She has always meant to do everything as soon as she's married. Then and then only she'll be safe. How will any one ever look at her if she makes herself a fright? How could she ever have got engaged if she had made herself a fright from the first? It's no use to insist that with her beauty she can never *be* a fright. She said to me this morning, poor girl, the most characteristic, the most harrowing things. 'My face is all I have—and *such* a face! I knew from the first I could do anything with it. But I needed it all—I need it still, every exquisite inch of it. It isn't as if I had a figure or anything else. Oh if God had only given me a figure too, I don't say! Yes, with a figure, a really good one, like Fanny Floyd-Taylor's, who's hideous, I'd have risked plain glasses. Que voulez-vous? No one is perfect.' She says she still has money left, but I don't believe a word of it. She has been speculating on her impunity, on the idea that her danger would hold off: she has literally been running a race with it. Her theory has been, as you from the first so clearly saw, that she'd get in ahead. She swears to me that though the 'bar' is too cruel she wears when she's alone what she has been ordered to wear. But when the deuce is she alone? It's herself of course that she has swindled worst: she has put herself off, so insanely that even her conceit but half accounts for it, with little inadequate concessions, little false measures and preposterous evasions and childish hopes. Her great terror is now that Iffield, who already has suspicions, who has found out her pince-nez but whom she has beguiled with some unblushing hocus-pocus, may discover the dreadful facts; and the essence of what she wanted this morning was in that interest to square me, to get me to deny indignantly and authoritatively (for isn't she my 'favourite sitter?') that she has anything in life the matter with any part of her. She sobbed, she 'went on,' she entreated; after we got talking her extraordinary nerve left her and she showed me what she has been through—showed me also all her terror of the harm I could do her. 'Wait till I'm married! wait till I'm married!' She took hold of me, she almost sank on her knees. It seems to me highly immoral, one's participation in her fraud; but there's no doubt that she must be married: I don't know what I don't see behind it! Therefore," I wound up, "Dawling must keep his hands off."

Mrs. Meldrum had held her breath; she gave out a long moan. "Well, that's exactly what I came here to tell him."

"Then here he is." Our host, all unprepared, his latchkey still in his hand, had just pushed open the door and, startled at finding us, turned a frightened look from one to the other, wondering what disaster we were there to announce or avert.

Mrs. Meldrum was on the spot all gaiety. "I've come to return your sweet visit. Ah," she laughed, "I mean to keep up the acquaintance!"

"Do—do," he murmured mechanically and absently, continuing to look at us. Then he broke out: "He's going to marry her."

I was surprised. "You already know?"

He produced an evening paper, which he tossed down on the table. "It's in that."

"Published—already?" I was still more surprised.

"Oh Flora can't keep a secret!"—Mrs. Meldrum made it light. She went up to poor Dawling and laid a motherly hand upon him.

"It's all right—it's just as it ought to be: don't think about her ever any more." Then as he met this adjuration with a stare from which thought, and of the most defiant and dismal, fairly protruded, the excellent woman put up her funny face and tenderly kissed him on the cheek.

CHAPTER X

I have spoken of these reminiscences as of a row of coloured beads, and I confess that as I continue to straighten out my chaplet I am rather proud of the comparison. The beads are all there, as I said—they slip along the string in their small smooth roundness. Geoffrey Dawling accepted as a gentleman the event his evening paper had proclaimed; in view of which I snatched a moment to nudge him a hint that he might offer Mrs. Meldrum his hand. He returned me a heavy head-shake, and I judged that marriage would henceforth strike him very much as the traffic of the street may strike some poor incurable at the window of an hospital. Circumstances arising at this time led to my making an absence from England, and circumstances already existing offered him a firm basis for similar action. He had after all the usual resource of a Briton—he could take to his boats, always drawn up in our background. He started on a journey round the globe, and I was left with nothing but my inference as to what might have happened. Later observation however only confirmed my belief that if at any time during the couple of months after Flora Saunt's brilliant engagement he had made up, as they say, to the good lady of Folkestone, that good lady would not have pushed him over the cliff. Strange as she was to behold I knew of cases in which she had been obliged to administer that shove. I went to New York to paint a couple of portraits; but I found, once on the spot, that I had counted without Chicago, where I was invited to blot out this harsh discrimination by the production of some dozen. I spent a year in America and should probably have spent a second had I not been summoned back to England by alarming news from my mother. Her strength had failed, and as soon as I reached London I hurried down to Folkestone, arriving just at the moment to offer a welcome to some slight symptom of a rally. She had been much worse but was now a little better; and though I found nothing but satisfaction in having come to her I saw after a few hours that my London studio, where arrears of work had already met me, would be my place to await whatever might next occur. Yet before returning to town I called on Mrs. Meldrum, from whom I had not had a line, and my view of whom, with the adjacent objects, as I had left them, had been intercepted by a luxuriant foreground.

Before I had gained her house I met her, as I supposed, coming toward me across the down, greeting me from afar with the familiar twinkle of her great vitreous badge; and as it was late in the autumn and the esplanade a blank I was free to acknowledge this signal by cutting a caper on the grass. My enthusiasm dropped indeed the next moment, for I had seen in a few more seconds that the person thus assaulted had by no means the figure of my military friend. I felt a shock much greater than any I should have thought possible when on this person's drawing near I knew her for poor little Flora Saunt. At what moment she had recognised me belonged to an order of mysteries over which, it quickly came home to me, one would never linger again: once we were face to face it so chiefly mattered that I should succeed in looking entirely unastonished. All I at first saw was the big gold bar crossing each of her lenses, over which something convex and grotesque, like the eyes of a large insect, something that now represented her whole personality, seemed, as out of the orifice of a prison, to strain forward and press. The face had shrunk away: it looked smaller, appeared even to look plain; it was at all events, so far as the effect on a spectator was concerned, wholly sacrificed to this huge apparatus of sight. There was no smile in it, and she made no motion to take my offered hand.

"I had no idea you were down here!" I said and I wondered whether she didn't know me at all or knew me only by my voice.

"You thought I was Mrs. Meldrum," she ever so quietly answered.

It was just this low pitch that made me protest with laughter. "Oh yes, you have a tremendous deal in common with Mrs. Meldrum! I've just returned to England after a long absence and I'm on my way to see her. Won't you come with me?" It struck me that her old reason for keeping clear of our friend was well disposed of now.

"I've just left her. I'm staying with her." She stood solemnly fixing me with her goggles. "Would you like to paint me now?" she asked. She seemed to speak, with intense gravity, from behind a mask or a cage.

There was nothing to do but treat the question still with high spirits. "It would be a fascinating little artistic problem!" That something was wrong it wasn't difficult to see, but a good deal more than met the eye might be presumed to be wrong if Flora was under Mrs. Meldrum's roof. I hadn't for a year had much time to think of her, but my imagination had had ground for lodging her in more gilded halls. One of the last things I had heard before leaving England was that in commemoration of the new relationship she had gone to stay with Lady Considine. This had made me take everything else for granted, and the noisy American world had deafened my care to possible contradictions. Her spectacles were at present a direct contradiction; they seemed a negation not only of new relationships but of every old one as well. I remember nevertheless that when after a moment she walked beside me on the grass I found myself nervously hoping she wouldn't as yet at any rate tell me anything very dreadful; so that to stave off this danger I harried her with questions about Mrs. Meldrum and, without waiting for replies, became profuse on the subject of my own doings. My companion was finely silent, and I felt both as if she were watching my nervousness with a sort of sinister irony and as if I were talking to some different and strange person. Flora plain and obscure and dumb was no Flora at all. At Mrs. Meldrum's door she turned off with the observation that as there was certainly a great deal I should have to say to our friend she had better not go in with me. I looked at her again—I had been keeping my eyes away from her—but only to meet her magnified stare. I greatly desired in truth to see Mrs. Meldrum alone, but there was something so grim in the girl's trouble that I hesitated to fall in with this idea of dropping her. Yet one couldn't express a compassion without seeming to take for granted more trouble than there actually might have been. I reflected that I must really figure to her as a fool, which was an entertainment I had never expected to give her. It rolled over me there for the first time—it has come back to me since—that there is, wondrously, in very deep and even in very foolish misfortune a dignity still finer than in the most inveterate habit of being all right. I couldn't have to her the manner of treating it as a mere detail that I was face to face with a part of what, at our last meeting, we had had such a scene about; but while I was trying to think of some manner that I *could* have she said quite colourlessly, though somehow as if she might never see me again: "Good-bye. I'm going to take my walk."

"All alone?"

She looked round the great bleak cliff-top. "With whom should I go? Besides I like to be alone—for the present."

This gave me the glimmer of a vision that she regarded her disfigurement as temporary, and the confidence came to me that she would never, for her happiness, cease to be a creature of illusions. It enabled me to exclaim, smiling brightly and feeling indeed idiotic: "Oh I shall see you again! But I hope you'll have a very pleasant walk."

"All my walks are pleasant, thank you—they do me such a lot of good." She was as quiet as a mouse, and her words seemed to me stupendous in their wisdom. "I take several a day," she continued. She might have been an ancient woman responding with humility at the church door to the patronage of the parson. "The more I take the better I feel. I'm ordered by the doctors to keep all the while in the air and go in for plenty of exercise. It keeps up my general health, you know, and if that goes on improving as it has lately done everything will soon be all right. All that was the matter with me before—and always; it was too reckless!—was that I neglected my general health. It acts directly on the state of the particular organ. So I'm going three miles."

I grinned at her from the doorstep while Mrs. Meldrum's maid stood there to admit me. "Oh I'm so glad," I said, looking at her as she paced away with the pretty flutter she had kept and remembering the day when, while she rejoined Lord Iffield, I had indulged in the same observation. Her air of assurance was on this occasion not less than it had been on that; but I recalled that she had then struck me as marching off to her doom. Was she really now marching away from it?

CHAPTER XI

As soon as I saw Mrs. Meldrum I of course broke out. "Is there anything in it? *Is* her general health—?"

Mrs. Meldrum checked me with her great amused blare. "You've already seen her and she has told you her wondrous tale? What's 'in it' is what has been in everything she has ever done—the most comical, tragical belief in herself. She thinks she's doing a 'cure.'"

"And what does her husband think?"

"Her husband? What husband?"

"Hasn't she then married Lord Iffield?"

"Vous-en-êtes là?" cried my hostess. "Why he behaved like a regular beast."

"How should I know? You never wrote me." Mrs. Meldrum hesitated, covering me with what poor Flora called the particular organ. "No, I didn't write you—I abstained on purpose. If I kept quiet I thought you mightn't hear over there what had happened. If you should hear I was afraid you would stir up Mr. Dawling."

"Stir him up?"

"Urge him to fly to the rescue; write out to him that there was another chance for him."

"I wouldn't have done it," I said.

"Well," Mrs. Meldrum replied, "it was not my business to give you an opportunity."

"In short you were afraid of it."

Again she hesitated and though it may have been only my fancy I thought she considerably reddened. At all events she laughed out. Then "I was afraid of it!" she very honestly answered.

"But doesn't he know? Has he given no sign?"

"Every sign in life—he came straight back to her. He did everything to get her to listen to him, but she hasn't the smallest idea of it."

"Has he seen her as she is now?" I presently and just a trifle awkwardly enquired.

"Indeed he has, and borne it like a hero. He told me all about it."

"How much you've all been through!" I found occasion to remark. "Then what has become of him?"

"He's at home in Hampshire. He has got back his old place and I believe by this time his old sisters. It's not half a bad little place."

"Yet its attractions say nothing to Flora?"

"Oh Flora's by no means on her back!" my fried declared.

"She's not on her back because she's on yours. Have you got her for the rest of your life?"

Once more Mrs. Meldrum genially glared. "Did she tell you how much the Hammond Synges have kindly left her to live on? Not quite eighty pounds a year."

"That's a good deal, but it won't pay the oculist. What was it that at last induced her to submit to him?"

"Her general collapse after that brute of an Iffield's rupture. She cried her eyes out—she passed through a horror of black darkness. Then came a gleam of light, and the light appears to have broadened. She went into goggles as repentant Magdalens go into the Catholic church."

"In spite of which you don't think she'll be saved?"

"*She* thinks she will—that's all I can tell you. There's no doubt that when once she brought herself to accept her real remedy, as she calls it, she began to enjoy a relief that she had never known. That feeling, very new and in spite of what she pays for it most refreshing, has given her something to hold on by, begotten in her foolish little mind a belief that, as she says, she's on the mend and that in the course of time, if she leads a tremendously healthy life, she'll be able to take off her muzzle and become as dangerous again as ever. It keeps her going."

"And what keeps you? You're good until the parties begin again."

"Oh she doesn't object to me now!" smiled Mrs. Meldrum. "I'm going to take her abroad; we shall be a pretty pair." I was struck with this energy and after a moment I enquired the reason of it. "It's to divert her mind," my friend replied, reddening again a little, I thought. "We shall go next week: I've only waited to see how your mother would be before starting." I expressed to her hereupon my sense of her extraordinary merit and also that of the inconceivability of Flora's fancying herself still in a situation not to jump at the chance of marrying a man like Dawling. "She says he's too ugly; she says he's too dreary; she says in fact he's 'nobody,'" Mrs. Meldrum pursued. "She says above all that he's not 'her own sort.' She doesn't deny that he's good, but she finds him impossibly ridiculous. He's quite the last person she would ever dream of." I was almost disposed on hearing this to protest that if the girl had so little proper feeling her noble suitor had perhaps served her right; but after a while my curiosity as to just how her noble suitor *had* served her got the better of that emotion, and I asked a question or two which led my companion again to apply to him the invidious term I have already quoted. What had happened was simply that Flora had at the eleventh hour broken down in the attempt to put him off with an uncandid account of her infirmity and that his lordship's interest in her had not been proof against the discovery of the way she had practised on him. Her dissimulation, he was obliged to perceive, had been infernally deep. The future in short assumed a new complexion for him when looked at through the grim glasses of a bride who, as he had said to some one, couldn't really, when you came to find out, see her hand before her face. He had conducted himself like any other jockeyed customer—he had returned the animal as unsound. He had backed out in his own way, giving the business, by some sharp shuffle, such a turn as to make the rupture ostensibly Flora's, but he had none the less remorselessly and basely backed out. He had cared for her lovely face, cared for it in the amused and haunted way it had been her poor little delusive gift to make men care; and her lovely face, damn it, with the monstrous gear she had begun to rig upon it, was just what had let him in. He had in the judgment of his family done everything that could be expected of him; he had made— Mrs. Meldrum had herself seen the letter—a "handsome" offer of pecuniary compensation. Oh if Flora, with her incredible buoyancy, was in a manner on her feet again now it was not that she had not for weeks and weeks been prone in the dust. Strange were the humiliations, the forms of anguish, it was given some natures to survive. That Flora had survived was perhaps after all a proof she was reserved for some final mercy. "But she has been in the abysses at any rate," said Mrs. Meldrum, "and I really don't think I can tell you what pulled her through."

"I think I can tell *you*," I returned. "What in the world but Mrs. Meldrum?"

At the end of an hour Flora had not come in, and I was obliged to announce that I should have but time to reach the station, where I was to find my luggage in charge of my mother's servant. Mrs. Meldrum put before me the question of waiting till a later train, so as not to lose our young lady, but I confess I gave this alternative a consideration less acute than I pretended. Somehow I didn't care if I did lose our young lady. Now that I knew the worst that had befallen her it struck me still less as possible to meet her on the ground of condolence; and with the sad appearance she wore to me what other ground was left? I lost her, but I caught my train. In truth she was so changed that one hated to see it; and now that she was in charitable hands one didn't feel compelled to make great efforts. I had studied her face for a particular beauty; I had lived with that beauty and reproduced it; but I knew what belonged to my trade well enough to be sure it was gone for ever.

CHAPTER XII

I was soon called back to Folkestone; but Mrs. Meldrum and her young friend had already left England, finding to that end every convenience on the spot and not having had to come up to town. My thoughts however were so painfully engaged there that I should in any case have had little attention for them: the event occurred that was to bring my series of visits to a close. When this high tide had ebbed I returned to America and to my interrupted work, which had opened out on such a scale that, with a deep plunge into a great chance, I was three good years in rising again to the surface. There are nymphs and naiads moreover in the American depths: they may have had something to do with the duration of my dive. I mention them to account for a grave misdemeanor—the fact that after the first year I rudely neglected Mrs. Meldrum. She had written to me from Florence after my mother's death and had mentioned in a postscript that in our young lady's calculations the lowest figures were now Italian counts. This was a good omen, and if in subsequent letters there was no news of a sequel I was content to accept small things and to believe that grave tidings, should there be any, would come to me in due course. The gravity of what might happen to a featherweight became indeed with time and distance less appreciable, and I was not without an impression that Mrs. Meldrum, whose sense of proportion was not the least of her merits, had no idea of boring the world with the ups and downs of her pensioner. The poor girl grew dusky and dim, a small fitful memory, a regret tempered by the comfortable consciousness of how kind Mrs. Meldrum would always be to her. I was professionally more preoccupied than I had ever been, and I had swarms of pretty faces in my eyes and a chorus of loud tones in my ears. Geoffrey Dawling had on his return to England written me two or three letters: his last information had been that he was going into the figures of rural illiteracy. I was delighted to receive it and had no doubt that if he should go into figures they would, as they are said to be able to prove anything, prove at least that my advice was sound and that he had wasted time enough. This quickened on my part another hope, a hope suggested by some roundabout rumour—I forget how it reached me—that he was engaged to a girl down in Hampshire. He turned out not to be, but I felt sure that if only he went into figures deep enough he would become, among the girls down in Hampshire or elsewhere, one of those numerous prizes of battle whose defences are practically not on the scale of their provocations. I nursed in short the thought that it was probably open to him to develop as one of the types about whom, as the years go on, superficial critics wonder without relief how they ever succeeded in dragging a bride to the altar. He never alluded to Flora Saunt; and there was in his silence about her, quite as in Mrs. Meldrum's, an element of instinctive tact, a brief implication that if you didn't happen to have been in love with her there was nothing to be said.

Within a week after my return to London I went to the opera, of which I had always been much of a devotee. I arrived too late for the first act of "Lohengrin," but the second was just beginning, and I gave myself up to it with no more than a glance at the house. When it was over I treated myself, with my glass, from my place in the stalls, to a general survey of the boxes, making doubtless on their contents the reflections, pointed by comparison, that are most familiar to the wanderer restored to London. There was the common sprinkling of pretty women, but I suddenly noted that one of these was far prettier than the others. This lady, alone in one of the smaller receptacles of the grand tier and already the aim of fifty tentative glasses, which she sustained with admirable serenity, this single exquisite figure, placed in the quarter furthest removed from my stall, was a person, I immediately felt, to cause one's curiosity to linger. Dressed in white, with diamonds in her hair and pearls on her neck, she had a pale radiance of beauty which even at that distance made her a distinguished presence and, with the air that easily attaches to lonely loveliness in public places, an agreeable mystery. A mystery however she remained to me only for a minute after I had levelled my glass at her: I feel to this moment the startled thrill, the shock almost of joy, with which I translated her vague brightness into a resurrection of Flora. I say a resurrection, because, to put it crudely, I had on that last occasion left our young woman for dead. At present perfectly alive again, she was altered only, as it were, by this fact of life. A little older, a little quieter, a little finer and a good deal fairer, she was simply transfigured by having recovered. Sustained by the reflection that even her recovery wouldn't enable her to distinguish me in the crowd, I was free to look at her well. Then it was it came home to me that my vision of her in her great goggles had been cruelly final. As her beauty was all there was of her, that machinery had extinguished her, and so far as I had thought of her in the interval I had thought of her as buried in the tomb her stern specialist had built. With the sense that she had escaped from it came a lively wish to return to her; and if I didn't straightway leave my place and rush round the theatre and up to her box it was because I was fixed to the spot some moments longer by the simple inability to cease looking at her.

She had been from the first of my seeing her practically motionless, leaning back in her chair with a kind of thoughtful grace and with her eyes vaguely directed, as it seemed on me, to one of the boxes on my side of the house and consequently over my head and out of my sight. The only movement she made for some time was to finger with an ungloved hand and as if with the habit of fondness the row of pearls on her neck, which my glass showed me to be large and splendid. Her diamonds and pearls, in her solitude, mystified me, making me, as she had had no such brave jewels in the days of the Hammond Synges, wonder what undreamt-of improvement had taken place in her fortunes. The ghost of a question hovered there a moment: could anything so prodigious have happened as that on her tested and proved amendment Lord Iffield had taken her back? This could scarce have without my hearing of it; and moreover if she had become a person of such fashion where was the little court one would naturally see at her elbow? Her isolation was puzzling, though it could easily suggest that she was but momentarily alone. If she had come with Mrs. Meldrum that lady would have taken advantage of the interval to pay a visit to some other box—doubtless the box at which Flora had just been looking. Mrs. Meldrum didn't account for the jewels, but the revival of Flora's beauty accounted for anything. She presently moved her eyes over the house, and I felt them brush me again like the wings of a dove. I don't know what quick pleasure flickered into the hope that she would at last see me. She did see me: she suddenly bent forward to take up the little double-barrelled ivory glass that rested on the edge of the box and to all appearance fix me with it. I smiled from my place straight up at the searching lenses, and after an instant she dropped them and smiled as straight back at me. Oh her smile—it was her old smile, her young smile, her very own smile made perfect! I instantly left my stall and hurried off for a nearer view of it; quite flushed, I remember, as I went with the annoyance of having happened to think of the idiotic way I had tried to paint her. Poor Iffield with his sample of that error, and still poorer Dawling in particular with *his*! I hadn't touched her, I was professionally humiliated, and as the attendant in the lobby opened her box for me I felt that the very first thing I should have to say to her would be that she must absolutely sit to me again.

CHAPTER XIII

She gave me the smile once more as over her shoulder, from her chair, she turned her face to me. "Here you are again!" she exclaimed with her disgloved hand put up a little backward for me to take. I dropped into a chair just behind her and, having taken it and noted that one of the curtains of the box would make the demonstration sufficiently private, bent my lips over it and impressed them on its finger-tips. It was given me however, to my astonishment, to feel next that all the privacy in the world couldn't have sufficed to mitigate the start with which she greeted this free application of my moustache: the blood had jumped to her face, she quickly recovered her hand and jerked at me, twisting herself round, a vacant challenging stare. During the next few instants several extraordinary things happened, the first of which was that now I was close to them the eyes of loveliness I had come up to look into didn't show at all the conscious light I had just been pleased to see them flash across the house: they showed on the contrary, to my confusion, a strange sweet blankness, an expression I failed to give a meaning to until, without delay, I felt on my arm, directed to it as if instantly to efface the effect of her start, the grasp of the hand she had impulsively snatched from me. It was the irrepressible question in this grasp that stopped on my lips all sound of salutation. She had mistaken my entrance for that of another person, a pair of lips without a moustache. She was feeling me to see who I was! With the perception of this and of her not seeing me I sat gaping at her and at the wild word that didn't come, the right word to express or to disguise my dismay. What was the right word to commemorate one's sudden discovery, at the very moment too at which one had been most encouraged to count on better things, that one's dear old friend had gone blind? Before the answer to this question dropped upon me—and the moving moments, though few, seemed many—I heard, with the sound of voices, the click of the attendant's key on the other side of the door. Poor Flora heard also and on hearing, still with her hand on my arm, brightened again as I had a minute since seen her brighten across the house: she had the sense of the return of the person she had taken me for—the person with the right pair of lips, as to whom I was for that matter much more in the dark than she. I gasped, but my word had come: if she had lost her sight it was in this very loss that she had found again her beauty. I managed to speak while we were still alone, before her companion had appeared. "You're lovelier at this day than you have ever been in your life!" At the sound of my voice and that of the opening of the door her impatience broke into audible joy. She sprang up, recognising me, always holding me, and gleefully cried to a gentleman who was arrested in the doorway by the sight of me: "He has come back, he has come back, and you should have heard what he says of me!" The gentleman was Geoffrey Dawling, and I thought it best to let him hear on the spot. "How beautiful she is, my dear man—but how extraordinarily beautiful! More beautiful at this hour than ever, ever before!"

It gave them almost equal pleasure and made Dawling blush to his eyes; while this in turn produced, in spite of deepened astonishment, a blest snap of the strain I had been struggling with. I wanted to embrace them both, and while the opening bars of another scene rose from the orchestra I almost did embrace Dawling, whose first emotion on beholding me had visibly and ever so oddly been a consciousness of guilt. I had caught him somehow in the act, though that was as yet all I knew; but by the time we sank noiselessly into our chairs again—for the music was supreme, Wagner passed first—my demonstration ought pretty well to have given him the limit of the criticism he had to fear. I myself indeed, while the opera blazed, was only too afraid he might divine in our silent closeness the very moral of my optimism, which was simply the comfort I had gathered from seeing that if our companion's beauty lived again her vanity partook of its life. I had hit on the right note—that was what eased me off: it drew all pain for the next half-hour from the sense of the deep darkness in which the stricken woman sat. If the music, in that darkness, happily soared and swelled for her, it beat its wings in unison with those of a gratified passion. A great deal came and went between us without profaning the occasion, so that I could feel at the end of twenty minutes as if I knew almost everything he might in kindness have to tell me; knew even why Flora, while I stared at her from the stalls, had misled me by the use of ivory and crystal and by appearing to recognise me and smile.

She leaned back in her chair in luxurious ease: I had from the first become aware that the way she fingered her pearls was a sharp image of the wedded state. Nothing of old had seemed wanting to her assurance, but I hadn't then dreamed of the art with which she would wear that assurance as a married woman. She had taken him when everything had failed; he had taken her when she herself had done so. His embarrassed eyes confessed it all, confessed the deep peace he found in it. They only didn't tell me why he had not written to me, nor clear up as yet a minor obscurity. Flora after a while again lifted the glass from the ledge of the box and elegantly swept the house with it. Then, by the mere instinct of her grace, a motion but half conscious, she inclined her head into the void with the sketch of a salute, producing, I could see, a perfect imitation of response to some homage. Dawling and I looked at each other again; the tears came into his eyes. She was playing at perfection still, and her misfortune only simplified the process.

I recognised that this was as near as I should ever come, certainly as I should come that night, to pressing on her misfortune. Neither of us would name it more than we were doing then, and Flora would never name it at all. Little by little I saw that what had occurred was, strange as it might appear, the best thing for her happiness. The question was now only of her beauty and her being seen and marvelled at; with Dawling to do for her everything in life her activity was limited to that. Such an activity was all within her scope; it asked nothing of her that she couldn't splendidly give. As from time to time in our delicate communion she turned her face to me with the parody of a look I lost none of the signs of its strange new glory. The expression of the eyes was a rub of pastel from a master's thumb; the whole head, stamped with a sort of showy suffering, had gained a fineness from what she had passed through. Yes, Flora was settled for life—nothing could hurt her further. I foresaw the particular praise she would mostly incur—she would be invariably "interesting." She would charm with her pathos more even than she had charmed with her pleasure. For herself above all she was fixed for ever, rescued from all change and ransomed from all doubt. Her old certainties, her old vanities were justified and sanctified, and in the darkness that had closed upon her one object remained clear. That object, as unfading as a mosaic mask, was fortunately the loveliest she could possibly look upon.

The greatest blessing of all was of course that Dawling thought so. Her future was ruled with the straightest line, and so for that matter was his. There were two facts to which before I left my friends I gave time to sink into my spirit. One was that he had changed by some process as effective as Flora's change, had been simplified somehow into service as she had been simplified into success. He was such a picture of inspired intervention as I had never yet conceived: he would exist henceforth for the sole purpose of rendering unnecessary, or rather impossible, any reference even on her own part to his wife's infirmity. Oh yes, how little desire he would ever give *me* to refer to it! He principally after a while made me feel—and this was my second lesson— that, good-natured as he was, my being there to see it all oppressed him; so that by the time the act ended I recognised that I too had filled out my hour. Dawling remembered things; I think he caught in my very face the irony of old judgments: they made him thresh about in his chair. I said to Flora as I took leave of her that I would come to see her, but I may mention that I never went. I'd go to-morrow if I hear she wants me; but what in the world can she ever want? As I quitted them I laid my hand on Dawling's arm, and drew him for a moment into the lobby.

"Why did you never write to me of your marriage?"

He smiled uncomfortably, showing his long yellow teeth and something more. "I don't know—the whole thing gave me such a tremendous lot to do."

This was the first dishonest speech I had heard him make: he really hadn't written because an idea that I would think him a still bigger fool than before. I didn't insist, but I tried there in the lobby, so far as a pressure of his hand could serve me, to give him a notion of what I thought him. "I can't at any rate make out," I said, "why I didn't hear from Mrs. Meldrum."

"She didn't write to you?"

"Never a word. What has become of her?"

"I think she's at Folkestone," Dawling returned; "but I'm sorry to say that practically she has ceased to see us."

"You haven't quarrelled with her?"

"How *could* we? Think of all we owe her. At the time of our marriage, and for months before, she did everything for us: I don't know how we should have managed without her. But since then she has never been near us and has given us rather markedly little encouragement to keep up relations with her."

I was struck with this, though of course I admit I am struck with all sorts of things. "Well," I said after a moment, "even if I could imagine a reason for that attitude it wouldn't explain why she shouldn't have taken account of my natural interest."

"Just so." Dawling's face was a windowless wall. He could contribute nothing to the mystery and, quitting him, I carried it away. It was not till I went down to ace Mrs. Meldrum that was really dispelled. She didn't want to hear of them or to talk of them, not a bit, and it was just in the same spirit that she hadn't wanted to write of them. She had done everything in the world for them, but now, thank heaven, the hard business was over. After I had taken this in, which I was quick to do, we quite avoided the subject. She simply couldn't bear it.

GREVILLE FANE

GREVILLE FANE.

COMING in to dress for dinner, I found a telegram: "Mrs. Stormer dying; can you give us half a column for to-morrow evening? Let her off easy, but not too easy." I was late; I was in a hurry; I had very little time to think, but at a venture I dispatched a reply: "Will do what I can." It was not till I had dressed and was rolling away to dinner that, in the hansom, I bethought myself of the difficulty of the condition attached. The difficulty was not of course in letting her off easy but in qualifying that indulgence. "I simply won't qualify it," I said to myself. I didn't admire her, but I liked her, and I had known her so long that I almost felt heartless in sitting down at such an hour to a feast of indifference. I must have seemed abstracted, for the early years of my acquaintance with her came back to me. I spoke of her to the lady I had taken down, but the lady I had taken down had never heard of Greville Fane. I tried my other neighbour, who pronounced her books "too vile." I had never thought them very good, but I should let her off easier than that.

I came away early, for the express purpose of driving to ask about her. The journey took time, for she lived in the north-west district, in the neighbourhood of Primrose Hill. My apprehension that I should be too late was justified in a fuller sense than I had attached to it—I had only feared that the house would be shut up. There were lights in the windows, and the temperate tinkle of my bell brought a servant immediately to the door, but poor Mrs. Stormer had passed into a state in which the resonance of no earthly knocker was to be feared. A lady, in the hall, hovering behind the servant, came forward when she heard my voice. I recognised Lady Luard, but she had mistaken me for the doctor.

"Excuse my appearing at such an hour," I said; "it was the first possible moment after I heard."

"It's all over," Lady Luard replied. "Dearest mamma!"

She stood there under the lamp with her eyes on me; she was very tall, very stiff, very cold, and always looked as if these things, and some others beside, in her dress, her manner and even her name, were an implication that she was very admirable. I had never been able to follow the argument, but that is a detail. I expressed briefly and frankly what I felt, while the little mottled maidservant flattened herself against the wall of the narrow passage and tried to look detached without looking indifferent. It was not a moment to make a visit, and I was on the point of retreating when Lady Luard arrested me with a queer, casual, drawling "Would you—a—would you, perhaps, be *writing* something?" I felt for the instant like an interviewer, which I was not. But I pleaded guilty to this intention, on which she rejoined: "I'm so very glad—but I think my brother would like to see you." I detested her brother, but it wasn't an occasion to act this out; so I suffered myself to be inducted, to my surprise, into a small back room which I immediately recognised as the scene, during the later years, of Mrs. Stormer's imperturbable industry. Her table was there, the battered and blotted accessory to innumerable literary lapses, with its contracted space for the arms (she wrote only from the elbow down) and the confusion of scrappy, scribbled sheets which had already become literary remains. Leolin was also there, smoking a cigarette before the fire and looking impudent even in his grief, sincere as it well might have been.

To meet him, to greet him, I had to make a sharp effort; for the air that he wore to me as he stood before me was quite that of his mother's murderer. She lay silent for ever upstairs—as dead as an unsuccessful book, and his swaggering erectness was a kind of symbol of his having killed her. I wondered if he had already, with his sister, been calculating what they could get for the poor papers on the table; but I had not long to wait to learn, for in reply to the scanty words of sympathy I addressed him he puffed out: "It's miserable, miserable, yes; but she has left three books complete." His words had the oddest effect; they converted the cramped little room into a seat of trade and made the "book" wonderfully feasible. He would certainly get all that could be got for the three. Lady Luard explained to me that her husband had been with them but had had to go down to the House. To her brother she explained that I was going to write something, and to me again she made it clear that she hoped I would "do mamma justice." She added that she didn't think this had ever been done. She said to her brother: "Don't you think there are some things he ought thoroughly to understand?" and on his instantly exclaiming "Oh, thoroughly—thoroughly!" she went on, rather austerely: "I mean about mamma's birth."

"Yes, and her connections," Leolin added.

I professed every willingness, and for five minutes I listened, but it would be too much to say that I understood. I don't even now, but it is not important. My vision was of other matters than those they put before me, and while they desired there should be no mistake about their ancestors I became more and more lucid about themselves. I got away as soon as possible, and walked home through the great dusky, empty London—the best of all conditions for thought. By the time I reached my door my little article was practically composed—ready to be transferred on the morrow from the polished plate of fancy. I believe it attracted some notice, was thought "graceful" and was said to be by some one else. I had to be pointed without being lively, and it took some tact. But what I said was much less interesting than what I thought—especially during the half-hour I spent in my armchair by the fire, smoking the cigar I always light before going to bed. I went to sleep there, I believe; but I continued to moralise about Greville Fane. I am reluctant to lose that retrospect altogether, and this is a dim little memory of it, a document not to "serve." The dear woman had written a hundred stories, but none so curious as her own.

When first I knew her she had published half-a-dozen fictions, and I believe I had also perpetrated a novel. She was more than a dozen years older than I, but she was a person who always acknowledged her relativity. It was not so very long ago, but in London, amid the big waves of the present, even a near horizon gets hidden. I met her at some dinner and took her down, rather flattered at offering my arm to a celebrity. She didn't look like one, with her matronly, mild, inanimate face, but I supposed her greatness would come out in her conversation. I gave it all the opportunities I could, but I was not disappointed when I found her only a dull, kind woman. This was why I liked her—she rested me so from literature. To myself literature was an irritation, a torment; but Greville Fane slumbered in the intellectual part of it like a Creole in a hammock. She was not a woman of genius, but her faculty was so special, so much a gift out of hand, that I have often wondered why she fell below that distinction. This was doubtless because the transaction, in her case, had remained incomplete; genius always pays for the gift, feels the debt, and she was placidly unconscious of obligation. She could invent stories by the yard, but she couldn't write a page of English. She went down to her grave without suspecting that though she had contributed volumes to the diversion of her contemporaries she had not contributed a sentence to the language. This had not prevented bushels of criticism from being heaped upon her head; she was worth a couple of columns any day to the weekly papers, in which it was shown that her pictures of life were dreadful but her style really charming. She asked me to come and see her, and I went. She lived then in Montpellier Square; which helped me to see how dissociated her imagination was from her character.

An industrious widow, devoted to her daily stint, to meeting the butcher and baker and making a home for her son and daughter, from the moment she took her pen in her hand she became a creature of passion. She thought the English novel deplorably wanting in that element, and the task she had cut out for herself was to supply the deficiency. Passion in high life was the general formula of this work, for her imagination was at home only in the most exalted circles. She adored, in truth, the aristocracy, and they constituted for her the romance of the world or, what is more to the point, the prime material of fiction. Their beauty and luxury, their loves and revenges, their temptations and surrenders, their immoralities and diamonds were as familiar to her as the blots on her writing-table. She was not a belated producer of the old fashioned novel, she had a cleverness and a modernness of her own, she had freshened up the fly-blown tinsel. She turned off plots by the hundred and—so far as her flying quill could convey her—was perpetually going abroad. Her types, her illustrations, her tone were nothing if not cosmopolitan. She recognised nothing less provincial than European society, and her fine folk knew each other and made love to each other from Doncaster to Bucharest. She had an idea that she resembled Balzac, and her favourite historical characters were Lucien de Rubempré and the Vidame de Pamiers. I must add that when I once asked her who the latter personage was she was unable to tell me. She was very brave and healthy and cheerful, very abundant and innocent and wicked. She was clever and vulgar and snobbish, and never so intensely British as when she was particularly foreign.

This combination of qualities had brought her early success, and I remember having heard with wonder and envy of what she "got," in those days, for a novel. The revelation gave me a pang: it was such a proof that, practising a totally different style, I should never make my fortune. And yet when, as I knew her better she told me her real tariff and I saw how rumour had quadrupled it, I liked her enough to be sorry. After a while I discovered too that if she got less it was not that *I* was to get any more. My failure never had what Mrs. Stormer would have called the banality of being relative—it was always admirably absolute. She lived at ease however in those days—ease is exactly the word, though she produced three novels a year. She scorned me when I spoke of difficulty—it was the only thing that made her angry. If I hinted that a work of art required a tremendous licking into shape she thought it a pretension and a *pose*. She never recognised the "torment of form"; the furthest she went was to introduce into one of her books (in satire her hand was heavy) a young poet who was always talking about it. I couldn't quite understand her irritation on this score, for she had nothing at stake in the matter. She had a shrewd perception that form, in prose at least, never recommended any one to the public we were condemned to address, and therefore she lost nothing (putting her private humiliation aside) by not having any. She made no pretence of producing works of art, but had comfortable tea-drinking hours in which she freely confessed herself a common pastrycook, dealing in such tarts and puddings as would bring customers to the shop. She put in plenty of sugar and of cochineal, or whatever it is that gives these articles a rich and attractive colour. She had a serene superiority to observation and opportunity which constituted an inexpugnable strength and would enable her to go on indefinitely. It is only real success that wanes, it is only solid things that melt. Greville Fane's ignorance of life was a resource still more unfailing than the most approved receipt. On her saying once that the day would come when she should have written herself out I answered: "Ah, you look into fairyland, and the fairies love you, and *they* never change. Fairyland is always there; it always was from the beginning of time, and it always will be to the end. They've given you the key and you can always open the door. With me it's different; I try, in my clumsy way, to be in some direct relation to life." "Oh, bother your direct relation to life!" she used to reply, for she was always annoyed by the phrase—which would not in the least prevent her from using it when she wished to try for style. With no more prejudices than an old sausage-mill, she would give forth again with patient punctuality any poor verbal scrap that had been dropped into her. I cheered her with saying that the dark day, at the end, would be for the like of *me*; inasmuch as, going in our small way by experience and observation, we depended not on a revelation, but on a little tiresome process. Observation depended on opportunity, and where should we be when opportunity failed?

One day she told me that as the novelist's life was so delightful and during the good years at least such a comfortable support (she had these staggering optimisms) she meant to train up her boy to follow it. She took the ingenious view that it was a profession like another and that therefore everything was to be gained by beginning young and serving an apprenticeship. Moreover the education would be less expensive than any other special course, inasmuch as she could administer it herself. She didn't profess to keep a school, but she could at least teach her own child. It was not that she was so very clever, but (she confessed to me as if she were afraid I would laugh at her) that *he* was. I didn't laugh at her for that, for I thought the boy sharp—I had seen him at sundry times. He was well grown and good-looking and unabashed, and both he and his sister made me wonder about their defunct papa, concerning whom the little I knew was that he had been a clergyman. I explained them to myself by suppositions and imputations possibly unjust to the departed; so little were they—superficially at least—the children of their mother. There used to be, on an easel in her drawing-room, an enlarged photograph of her husband, done by some horrible posthumous "process" and draped, as to its florid frame, with a silken scarf, which testified to the candour of Greville Fane's bad taste. It made him look like an unsuccessful tragedian; but it was not a thing to trust. He may have been a successful comedian. Of the two children the girl was the elder, and struck me in all her younger years as singularly colourless. She was only very long, like an undecipherable letter.

It was not till Mrs. Stormer came back from a protracted residence abroad that Ethel (which was this young lady's name) began to produce the effect, which was afterwards remarkable in her, of a certain kind of high resolution. She made one apprehend that she meant to do something for herself. She was long-necked and near-sighted and striking, and I thought I had never seen sweet seventeen in a form so hard and high and dry. She was cold and affected and ambitious, and she carried an eyeglass with a long handle, which she put up whenever she wanted not to see. She had come out, as the phrase is, immensely; and yet I felt as if she were surrounded with a spiked iron railing. What she meant to do for herself was to marry, and it was the only thing, I think, that she meant to do for any one else; yet who would be inspired to clamber over that bristling barrier? What flower of tenderness or of intimacy would such an adventurer conceive as his reward?

This was for Sir Baldwin Luard to say; but he naturally never confided to me the secret. He was a joyless, jokeless young man, with the air of having other secrets as well, and a determination to get on politically that was indicated by his never having been known to commit himself—as regards any proposition whatever—beyond an exclamatory "Oh!" His wife and he must have conversed mainly in prim ejaculations, but they understood sufficiently that they were kindred spirits. I remember being angry with Greville Fane when she announced these nuptials to me as magnificent; I remember asking her what splendour there was in the union of the daughter of a woman of genius with an irredeemable mediocrity. "Oh! he's awfully clever," she said; but she blushed for the maternal fib. What she meant was that though Sir Baldwin's estates were not vast (he had a dreary house in South Kensington and a still drearier "Hall" somewhere in Essex, which was let), the connection was a "smarter" one than a child of hers could have aspired to form. In spite of the social bravery of her novels she took a very humble and dingy view of herself, so that of all her productions "my daughter Lady Luard" was quite the one she was proudest of. That personage thought her mother very vulgar and was distressed and perplexed by the occasional license of her pen, but had a complicated attitude in regard to this indirect connection with literature. So far as it was lucrative her ladyship approved of it, and could compound with the inferiority of the pursuit by doing practical justice to some of its advantages. I had reason to know (my reason was simply that poor Mrs. Stormer told me) that she suffered the inky fingers to press an occasional bank-note into her palm. On the other hand she deplored the "peculiar style" to which Greville Fane had devoted herself, and wondered where an author who had the convenience of so lady-like a daughter could have picked up such views about the best society. "She might know better, with Leolin and me," Lady Luard had been known to remark; but it appeared that some of Greville Fane's superstitions were incurable. She didn't live in Lady Luard's society, and the best was not good enough for her—she must make it still better.

I could see that this necessity grew upon her during the years she spent abroad, when I had glimpses of her in the shifting sojourns that lay in the path of my annual ramble. She betook herself from Germany to Switzerland and from Switzerland to Italy; she favoured cheap places and set up her desk in the smaller capitals. I took a look at her whenever I could, and I always asked how Leolin was getting on. She gave me beautiful accounts of him, and whenever it was possible the boy was produced for my edification. I had entered from the first into the joke of his career—I pretended to regard him as a consecrated child. It had been a joke for Mrs. Stormer at first, but the boy himself had been shrewd enough to make the matter serious. If his mother accepted the principle that the intending novelist cannot begin too early to see life, Leolin was not interested in hanging back from the application of it. He was eager to qualify himself, and took to cigarettes at ten, on the highest literary grounds. His poor mother gazed at him with extravagant envy and, like Desdemona, wished heaven had made *her* such a man. She explained to me more than once that in her profession she had found her sex a dreadful drawback. She loved the story of Madame George Sand's early rebellion against this hindrance, and believed that if she had worn trousers she could have written as well as that lady. Leolin had for the career at least the qualification of trousers, and as he grew older he recognised its importance by laying in an immense assortment. He grew up in gorgeous apparel, which was his way of interpreting his mother's system. Whenever I met her I found her still under the impression that she was carrying this system out and that Leolin's training was bearing fruit. She was giving him experience, she was giving him impressions, she was putting a *gagnepain* into his hand. It was another name for spoiling him with the best conscience in the world. The queerest pictures come back to me of this period of the good lady's life and of the extraordinarily virtuous, muddled, bewildering tenor of it. She had an idea that she was seeing foreign manners as well as her petticoats would allow; but, in reality she was not seeing anything, least of all fortunately how much she was laughed at. She drove her whimsical pen at Dresden and at Florence, and produced in all places and at all times the same romantic and ridiculous fictions. She carried about her box of properties and fished out promptly the familiar, tarnished old puppets. She believed in them when others couldn't, and as they were like nothing that was to be seen under the sun it was impossible to prove by comparison that they were wrong. You can't compare birds and fishes; you could only feel that, as Greville Fane's characters had the fine plumage of the former species, human beings must be of the latter.

It would have been droll if it had not been so exemplary to see her tracing the loves of the duchesses beside the innocent cribs of her children. The immoral and the maternal lived together in her diligent days on the most comfortable terms, and she stopped curling the mustaches of her Guardsmen to pat the heads of her babes. She was haunted by solemn spinsters who came to tea from continental *pensions*, and by unsophisticated Americans who told her she was just loved in *their* country. "I had rather be just paid there," she usually replied; for this tribute of transatlantic opinion was the only thing that galled her. The Americans went away thinking her coarse; though as the author of so many beautiful love-stories she was disappointing to most of these pilgrims, who had not expected to find a shy, stout, ruddy lady in a cap like a crumbled pyramid. She wrote about the affections and the impossibility of controlling them, but she talked of the price of *pension* and the convenience of an English chemist. She devoted much thought and many thousands of francs to the education of her daughter, who spent three years at a very superior school at Dresden, receiving wonderful instruction in sciences, arts and tongues, and who, taking a different line from Leolin, was to be brought up wholly as a *femme du monde*. The girl was musical and philological; she made a specialty of languages and learned enough about them to be inspired with a great contempt for her mother's artless accents. Greville Fane's French and Italian were droll; the imitative faculty had been denied her, and she had an unequalled gift, especially pen in hand, of squeezing big mistakes into small opportunities. She knew it, but she didn't care; correctness was the virtue in the world that, like her heroes and heroines, she valued least. Ethel, who had perceived in her pages some remarkable lapses, undertook at one time to revise her proofs; but I remember her telling me a year after the girl had left school that this function had been very briefly exercised. "She can't read me," said Mrs. Stormer; "I offend her taste. She tells me that at Dresden— at school—I was never allowed." The good lady seemed surprised at this, having the best conscience in the world about her lucubrations. She had never meant to fly in the face of anything, and considered that she grovelled before the Rhadamanthus of the English literary tribunal, the celebrated and awful Young Person. I assured her, as a joke, that she was frightfully indecent (she hadn't in fact that reality any more than any other) my purpose being solely to prevent her from guessing that her daughter had dropped her not because she was immoral but because she was vulgar. I used to figure her children closeted together and asking each other while they exchanged a gaze of dismay: "Why should she *be* so—and so *fearfully* so—when she has the advantage of our society? Shouldn't *we* have taught her better?" Then I imagined their recognising with a blush and a shrug that she was unteachable, irreformable. Indeed she was, poor lady; but it is never fair to read by the light of taste things that were not written by it. Greville Fane had, in the topsy-turvy, a serene good faith that ought to have been safe from allusion, like a stutter or a *faux pas*.

She didn't make her son ashamed of the profession to which he was destined, however; she only made him ashamed of the way she herself exercised it. But he bore his humiliation much better than his sister, for he was ready to take for granted that he should one day restore the balance. He was a canny and far-seeing youth, with appetites and aspirations, and he had not a scruple in his composition. His mother's theory of the happy knack he could pick up deprived him of the wholesome discipline required to prevent young idlers from becoming cads. He had, abroad, a casual tutor and a snatch or two of a Swiss school, but no consecutive study, no prospect of a university or a degree. It may be imagined with what zeal, as the years went on, he entered into the pleasantry of there being no manual so important to him as the massive book of life. It was an expensive volume to peruse, but Mrs. Stormer was willing to lay out a sum in what she would have called her *premiers frais*. Ethel disapproved—she thought this education far too unconventional for an English gentleman. Her voice was for Eton and Oxford, or for any public school (she would have resigned herself) with the army to follow. But Leolin never was afraid of his sister, and they visibly disliked, though they sometimes agreed to assist, each other. They could combine to work the oracle—to keep their mother at her desk.

When she came back to England, telling me she had got all the continent could give her, Leolin was a broad-shouldered, red-faced young man, with an immense wardrobe and an extraordinary assurance of manner. She was fondly obstinate about her having taken the right course with him, and proud of all that he knew and had seen. He was now quite ready to begin, and a little while later she told me he *had* begun. He had written something tremendously clever, and it was coming out in the *Cheapside*. I believe it came out; I had no time to look for it; I never heard anything about it. I took for granted that if this contribution had passed through his mother's hands it had practically become a specimen of her own genius, and it was interesting to consider Mrs. Stormer's future in the light of her having to write her son's novels as well as her own. This was not the way she looked at it herself; she took the charming ground that he would help her to write hers. She used to tell me that he supplied passages of the greatest value to her own work—all sorts of technical things, about hunting and yachting and wine—that she couldn't be expected to get very straight. It was all so much practice for him and so much alleviation for her. I was unable to identify these pages, for I had long since ceased to "keep up" with Greville Fane; but I was quite able to believe that the wine-question had been put, by Leolin's good offices, on a better footing, for the dear lady used to mix her drinks (she was perpetually serving the most splendid suppers) in the queerest fashion. I could see that he was willing enough to accept a commission to look after that department. It occurred to me indeed, when Mrs. Stormer settled in England again, that by making a shrewd use of both her children she might be able to rejuvenate her style. Ethel had come back to gratify her young ambition, and if she couldn't take her mother into society she would at least go into it herself. Silently, stiffly, almost grimly, this young lady held up her head, clenched her long teeth, squared her lean elbows and made her way up the staircases she had elected. The only communication she ever made to me, the only effusion of confidence with which she ever honoured me, was when she said: "I don't want to know the people mamma knows; I mean to know others." I took due note of the remark, for I was not one of the "others." I couldn't trace therefore the steps of her process; I could only admire it at a distance and congratulate her mother on the results. The results were that Ethel went to "big" parties and got people to take her. Some of them were people she had met abroad, and others were people whom the people she had met abroad had met. They ministered alike to Miss Ethel's convenience, and I wondered how she extracted so many favours without the expenditure of a smile. Her smile was the dimmest thing in the world, diluted lemonade, without sugar, and she had arrived precociously at social wisdom, recognising that if she was neither pretty enough nor rich enough nor clever enough, she could at least in her muscular youth be rude enough. Therefore if she was able to tell her mother what really took place in the mansions of the great, give her notes to work from, the quill could be driven at home to better purpose and precisely at a moment when it would have to be more active than ever. But if she did tell, it would appear that poor Mrs. Stormer didn't believe. As regards many points this was not a wonder; at any rate I heard nothing of Greville Fane's having developed a new manner. She had only one manner from start to finish, as Leolin would have said.

She was tired at last, but she mentioned to me that she couldn't afford to pause. She continued to speak of Leolin's work as the great hope of their future (she had saved no money) though the young man wore to my sense an aspect more and more professional if you like, but less and less literary. At the end of a couple of years there was something monstrous in the impudence with which he played his part in the comedy. When I wondered how she could play *her* part I had to perceive that her good faith was complete and that what kept it so was simply her extravagant fondness. She loved the young impostor with a simple, blind, benighted love, and of all the heroes of romance who had passed before her eyes he was by far the most brilliant.

He was at any rate the most real—she could touch him, pay for him, suffer for him, worship him. He made her think of her princes and dukes, and when she wished to fix these figures in her mind's eye she thought of her boy. She had often told me she was carried away by her own creations, and she was certainly carried away by Leolin. He vivified, by potentialities at least, the whole question of youth and passion. She held, not unjustly, that the sincere novelist should feel the whole flood of life; she acknowledged with regret that she had not had time to feel it herself, and it was a joy to her that the deficiency might be supplied by the sight of the way it was rushing through this magnificent young man. She exhorted him, I suppose, to let it rush; she wrung her own flaccid little sponge into the torrent. I knew not what passed between them in her hours of tuition, but I gathered that she mainly impressed on him that the great thing was to live, because that gave you material. He asked nothing better; he collected material, and the formula served as a universal pretext. You had only to look at him to see that, with his rings and breastpins, his cross-barred jackets, his early *embonpoint*, his eyes that looked like imitation jewels, his various indications of a dense, full-blown temperament, his idea of life was singularly vulgar; but he was not so far wrong as that his response to his mother's expectations was not in a high degree practical. If she had imposed a profession on him from his tenderest years it was exactly a profession that he followed. The two were not quite the same, inasmuch as *his* was simply to live at her expense; but at least she couldn't say that he hadn't taken a line. If she insisted on believing in him he offered himself to the sacrifice. My impression is that her secret dream was that he should have a *liaison* with a countess, and he persuaded her without difficulty that he had one. I don't know what countesses are capable of, but I have a clear notion of what Leolin was.

He didn't persuade his sister, who despised him—she wished to work her mother in her own way, and I asked myself why the girl's judgment of him didn't make me like her better. It was because it didn't save her after all from a mute agreement with him to go halves. There were moments when I couldn't help looking hard into his atrocious young eyes, challenging him to confess his fantastic fraud and give it up. Not a little tacit conversation passed between us in this way, but he had always the best of it. If I said: "Oh, come now, with *me* you needn't keep it up; plead guilty, and I'll let you off," he wore the most ingenuous, the most candid expression, in the depths of which I could read: "Oh, yes, I know it exasperates you—that's just why I do it." He took the line of earnest inquiry, talked about Balzac and Flaubert, asked me if I thought Dickens *did* exaggerate and Thackeray *ought* to be called a pessimist. Once he came to see me, at his mother's suggestion he declared, on purpose to ask me how far, in my opinion, in the English novel, one really might venture to "go." He was not resigned to the usual pruderies—he suffered under them already. He struck out the brilliant idea that nobody knew how far we might go, for nobody had ever tried. Did I think *he* might safely try—would it injure his mother if he did? He would rather disgrace himself by his timidities than injure his mother, but certainly some one ought to try. Wouldn't *I* try—couldn't I be prevailed upon to look at it as a duty? Surely the ultimate point ought to be fixed—he was worried, haunted by the question. He patronised me unblushingly, made me feel like a foolish amateur, a helpless novice, inquired into my habits of work and conveyed to me that I was utterly *vieux jeu* and had not had the advantage of an early training. I had not been brought up from the germ, I knew nothing of life—didn't go at it on *his* system. He had dipped into French feuilletons and picked up plenty of phrases, and he made a much better show in talk than his poor mother, who never had time to read anything and could only be vivid with her pen. If I didn't kick him downstairs it was because he would have alighted on her at the bottom.

When she went to live at Primrose Hill I called upon her and found her weary and wasted. It had waned a good deal, the elation caused the year before by Ethel's marriage; the foam on the cup had subsided and there was a bitterness in the draught.

She had had to take a cheaper house and she had to work still harder to pay even for that. Sir Baldwin was obliged to be close; his charges were fearful, and the dream of her living with her daughter (a vision she had never mentioned to me) must be renounced. "I would have helped with things, and I could have lived perfectly in one room," she said; "I would have paid for everything, and—after all—I'm some one, ain't I? But I don't fit in, and Ethel tells me there are tiresome people she *must* receive. I can help them from here, no doubt, better than from there. She told me once, you know, what she thinks of my picture of life. 'Mamma, your picture of life is preposterous!' No doubt it is, but she's vexed with me for letting my prices go down; and I had to write three novels to pay for all her marriage cost me. I did it very well—I mean the outfit and the wedding; but that's why I'm here. At any rate she doesn't want a dingy old woman in her house. I should give it an atmosphere of literary glory, but literary glory is only the eminence of nobodies. Besides, she doubts my glory—she knows I'm glorious only at Peckham and Hackney. She doesn't want her friends to ask if I've never known nice people. She can't tell them I've never been in society. She tried to teach me better once, but I couldn't learn. It would seem too as if Peckham and Hackney had had enough of me; for (don't tell any one!) I've had to take less for my last than I ever took for anything." I asked her how little this had been, not from curiosity, but in order to upbraid her, more disinterestedly than Lady Luard had done, for such concessions. She answered "I'm ashamed to tell you," and then she began to cry.

I had never seen her break down, and I was proportionately moved; she sobbed, like a frightened child, over the extinction of her vogue and the exhaustion of her vein. Her little workroom seemed indeed a barren place to grow flowers, and I wondered, in the after years (for she continued to produce and publish) by what desperate and heroic process she dragged them out of the soil. I remember asking her on that occasion what had become of Leolin, and how much longer she intended to allow him to amuse himself at her cost. She rejoined with spirit, wiping her eyes, that he was down at Brighton hard at work—he was in the midst of a novel—and that he *felt* life so, in all its misery and mystery, that it was cruel to speak of such experiences as a pleasure. "He goes beneath the surface," she said, "and he *forces* himself to look at things from which he would rather turn away. Do you call that amusing yourself? You should see his face sometimes! And he does it for me as much as for himself. He tells me everything—he comes home to me with his *trouvailles*. We are artists together, and to the artist all things are pure. I've often heard you say so yourself." The novel that Leolin was engaged in at Brighton was never published, but a friend of mine and of Mrs. Stormer's who was staying there happened to mention to me later that he had seen the young apprentice to fiction driving, in a dogcart, a young lady with a very pink face. When I suggested that she was perhaps a woman of title with whom he was conscientiously flirting my informant replied: "She is indeed, but do you know what her title is?" He pronounced it—it was familiar and descriptive—but I won't reproduce it here. I don't know whether Leolin mentioned it to his mother: she would have needed all the purity of the artist to forgive him. I hated so to come across him that in the very last years I went rarely to see her, though I knew that she had come pretty well to the end of her rope. I didn't want her to tell me that she had fairly to give her books away—I didn't want to see her cry. She kept it up amazingly, and every few months, at my club, I saw three new volumes, in green, in crimson, in blue, on the book-table that groaned with light literature. Once I met her at the Academy soirée, where you meet people you thought were dead, and she vouchsafed the information, as if she owed it to me in candour, that Leolin had been obliged to recognise insuperable difficulties in the question of *form*, he was so fastidious; so that she had now arrived at a definite understanding with him (it was such a comfort) that *she* would do the form if he would bring home the substance. That was now his position—he foraged for her in the great world at a salary. "He's my 'devil,' don't you see? as if I were a great lawyer: he gets up the case and I argue it." She mentioned further that in addition to his salary he was paid by the piece: he got so much for a striking character, so much for a pretty name, so much for a plot, so much for an incident, and had so much promised him if he would invent a new crime.

"He *has* invented one," I said, "and he's paid every day of his life."

"What is it?" she asked, looking hard at the picture of the year; "Baby's Tub," near which we happened to be standing.

I hesitated a moment. "I myself will write a little story about it, and then you'll see."

But she never saw; she had never seen anything, and she passed away with her fine blindness unimpaired. Her son published every scrap of scribbled paper that could be extracted from her table-drawers, and his sister quarrelled with him mortally about the proceeds, which showed that she only wanted a pretext, for they cannot have been great. I don't know what Leolin lives upon, unless it be on a queer lady many years older than himself, whom he lately married. The last time I met him he said to me with his infuriating smile: "Don't you think we can go a little further still—just a little?" *He* really goes too far.

About Author

Henry James OM (15 April 1843 – 28 February 1916) was an American-British author regarded as a key transitional figure between literary realism and literary modernism, and is considered by many to be among the greatest novelists in the English language. He was the son of Henry James Sr. and the brother of renowned philosopher and psychologist William James and diarist Alice James.

He is best known for a number of novels dealing with the social and marital interplay between émigré Americans, English people, and continental Europeans. Examples of such novels include The Portrait of a Lady, The Ambassadors, and The Wings of the Dove. His later works were increasingly experimental. In describing the internal states of mind and social dynamics of his characters, James often made use of a style in which ambiguous or contradictory motives and impressions were overlaid or juxtaposed in the discussion of a character's psyche. For their unique ambiguity, as well as for other aspects of their composition, his late works have been compared to impressionist painting.

His novella The Turn of the Screw has garnered a reputation as the most analysed and ambiguous ghost story in the English language and remains his most widely adapted work in other media. He also wrote a number of other highly regarded ghost stories and is considered one of the greatest masters of the field.

James published articles and books of criticism, travel, biography, autobiography, and plays. Born in the United States, James largely relocated to Europe as a young man and eventually settled in England, becoming a British subject in 1915, one year before his death. James was nominated for the Nobel Prize in Literature in 1911, 1912 and 1916.

Life

Early years, 1843–1883

James was born at 2 Washington Place in New York City on 15 April 1843. His parents were Mary Walsh and Henry James Sr. His father was intelligent and steadfastly congenial. He was a lecturer and philosopher who had inherited independent means from his father, an Albany banker and investor. Mary came from a wealthy family long settled in New York City. Her sister Katherine lived with her adult family for an extended period of time. Henry Jr. had three brothers, William, who was one year his senior, and younger brothers Wilkinson (Wilkie) and Robertson. His younger sister was Alice. Both of his parents were of Irish and Scottish descent.

The family first lived in Albany, at 70 N. Pearl St., and then moved to Fourteenth Street in New York City when James was still a young boy. His education was calculated by his father to expose him to many influences, primarily scientific and philosophical; it was described by Percy Lubbock, the editor of his selected letters, as "extraordinarily haphazard and promiscuous." James did not share the usual education in Latin and Greek classics. Between 1855 and 1860, the James' household traveled to London, Paris, Geneva, Boulogne-sur-Mer and Newport, Rhode Island, according to the father's current interests and publishing ventures, retreating to the United States when funds were low. Henry studied primarily with tutors and briefly attended schools while the family traveled in Europe. Their longest stays were in France, where Henry began to feel at home and became fluent in French. He was afflicted with a stutter, which seems to have manifested itself only when he spoke English; in French, he did not stutter.

In 1860 the family returned to Newport. There Henry became a friend of the painter John La Farge, who introduced him to French literature, and in particular, to Balzac. James later called Balzac his "greatest master," and said that he had learned more about the craft of fiction from him than from anyone else.

In the autumn of 1861 Henry received an injury, probably to his back, while fighting a fire. This injury, which resurfaced at times throughout his life, made him unfit for military service in the American Civil War.

In 1864 the James family moved to Boston, Massachusetts to be near William, who had enrolled first in the Lawrence Scientific School at Harvard and then in the medical school. In 1862 Henry attended Harvard Law School, but realised that he was not interested in studying law. He pursued his interest in literature and associated with authors and critics William Dean Howells and Charles Eliot Norton in Boston and Cambridge, formed lifelong friendships with Oliver Wendell Holmes Jr., the future Supreme Court Justice, and with James and Annie Fields, his first professional mentors.

His first published work was a review of a stage performance, "Miss Maggie Mitchell in Fanchon the Cricket," published in 1863. About a year later, A Tragedy of Error, his first short story, was published anonymously. James's first payment was for an appreciation of Sir Walter Scott's novels, written for the North American Review. He wrote fiction and non-fiction pieces for The Nation and Atlantic Monthly, where Fields was editor. In 1871 he published his first novel, Watch and Ward, in serial form in the Atlantic Monthly. The novel was later published in book form in 1878.

During a 14-month trip through Europe in 1869–70 he met Ruskin, Dickens, Matthew Arnold, William Morris, and George Eliot. Rome impressed him profoundly. "Here I am then in the Eternal City," he wrote to his brother William. "At last—for the first time—I live!" He attempted to support himself as a freelance writer in Rome, then secured a position as Paris correspondent for the New York Tribune, through the influence of its editor John Hay. When these efforts failed he returned to New York City. During 1874 and 1875 he published Transatlantic Sketches, A Passionate Pilgrim, and Roderick Hudson. During this early period in his career he was influenced by Nathaniel Hawthorne.

In 1869 he settled in London. There he established relationships with Macmillan and other publishers, who paid for serial installments that they would later publish in book form. The audience for these serialized novels was largely made up of middle-class women, and James struggled to fashion serious literary work within the strictures imposed by editors' and publishers' notions of what was suitable for young women to read. He lived in rented rooms but was able to join gentlemen's clubs that had libraries and where he could entertain male friends. He was introduced to English society by Henry Adams and Charles Milnes Gaskell, the latter introducing him to the Travellers' and the Reform Clubs.

In the fall of 1875 he moved to the Latin Quarter of Paris. Aside from two trips to America, he spent the next three decades—the rest of his life—in Europe. In Paris he met Zola, Alphonse Daudet, Maupassant, Turgenev, and others. He stayed in Paris only a year before moving to London.

In England he met the leading figures of politics and culture. He continued to be a prolific writer, producing The American (1877), The Europeans (1878), a revision of Watch and Ward (1878), French Poets and Novelists (1878), Hawthorne (1879), and several shorter works of fiction. In 1878 Daisy Miller established his fame on both sides of the Atlantic. It drew notice perhaps mostly because it depicted a woman whose behavior is outside the social norms of Europe. He also began his first masterpiece, The Portrait of a Lady, which would appear in 1881.

In 1877 he first visited Wenlock Abbey in Shropshire, home of his friend Charles Milnes Gaskell whom he had met through Henry Adams. He was much inspired by the darkly romantic Abbey and the surrounding countryside, which features in his essay Abbeys and Castles. In particular the gloomy monastic fishponds behind the Abbey are said to have inspired the lake in The Turn of the Screw.

While living in London, James continued to follow the careers of the "French realists", Émile Zola in particular. Their stylistic methods influenced his own work in the years to come. Hawthorne's influence on him faded during this period, replaced by George Eliot and Ivan Turgenev. 1879–1882 saw the publication of The Europeans, Washington Square, Confidence, and The Portrait of a Lady. He visited America in 1882–1883, then returned to London.

The period from 1881 to 1883 was marked by several losses. His mother died in 1881, followed by his father a few months later, and then by his brother Wilkie. Emerson, an old family friend, died in 1882. His friend Turgenev died in 1883.

Middle years, 1884–1897

In 1884 James made another visit to Paris. There he met again with Zola, Daudet, and Goncourt. He had been following the careers of the French "realist" or "naturalist" writers, and was increasingly influenced by them. In 1886, he published The Bostonians and The Princess Casamassima, both influenced by the French writers he'd studied assiduously. Critical reaction and sales were poor. He wrote to Howells that the books had hurt his career rather than helped because they had "reduced the desire, and demand, for my productions to zero". During this time he became friends with Robert Louis Stevenson, John Singer Sargent, Edmund Gosse, George du Maurier, Paul Bourget, and Constance Fenimore Woolson. His third novel from the 1880s was The Tragic Muse. Although he was following the precepts of Zola in his novels of the '80s, their tone and attitude are closer to the fiction of Alphonse Daudet. The lack of critical and financial success for his novels during this period led him to try writing for the theatre. (His dramatic works and his experiences with theatre are discussed below.)

In the last quarter of 1889, he started translating "for pure and copious lucre" Port Tarascon, the third volume of Alphonse Daudet adventures of Tartarin de Tarascon. Serialized in Harper's Monthly Magazine from June 1890, this translation praised as "clever" by The Spectator was published in January 1891 by Sampson Low, Marston, Searle & Rivington.

After the stage failure of Guy Domville in 1895, James was near despair and thoughts of death plagued him. The years spent on dramatic works were not entirely a loss. As he moved into the last phase of his career he found ways to adapt dramatic techniques into the novel form.

In the late 1880s and throughout the 1890s James made several trips through Europe. He spent a long stay in Italy in 1887. In that year the short novel The Aspern Papers and The Reverberator were published.

Late years, 1898–1916

In 1897–1898 he moved to Rye, Sussex, and wrote The Turn of the Screw. 1899–1900 saw the publication of The Awkward Age and The Sacred

Fount. During 1902–1904 he wrote The Ambassadors, The Wings of the Dove, and The Golden Bowl.

In 1904 he revisited America and lectured on Balzac. In 1906–1910 he published The American Scene and edited the "New York Edition", a 24-volume collection of his works. In 1910 his brother William died; Henry had just joined William from an unsuccessful search for relief in Europe on what then turned out to be his (Henry's) last visit to the United States (from summer 1910 to July 1911), and was near him, according to a letter he wrote, when he died.

In 1913 he wrote his autobiographies, A Small Boy and Others, and Notes of a Son and Brother. After the outbreak of the First World War in 1914 he did war work. In 1915 he became a British subject and was awarded the Order of Merit the following year. He died on 28 February 1916, in Chelsea, London. As he requested, his ashes were buried in Cambridge Cemetery in Massachusetts.

Biographers

James regularly rejected suggestions that he should marry, and after settling in London proclaimed himself "a bachelor". F. W. Dupee, in several volumes on the James family, originated the theory that he had been in love with his cousin Mary ("Minnie") Temple, but that a neurotic fear of sex kept him from admitting such affections: "James's invalidism ... was itself the symptom of some fear of or scruple against sexual love on his part." Dupee used an episode from James's memoir A Small Boy and Others, recounting a dream of a Napoleonic image in the Louvre, to exemplify James's romanticism about Europe, a Napoleonic fantasy into which he fled.

Dupee had not had access to the James family papers and worked principally from James's published memoir of his older brother, William, and the limited collection of letters edited by Percy Lubbock, heavily weighted toward James's last years. His account therefore moved directly from James's childhood, when he trailed after his older brother, to elderly invalidism. As more material became available to scholars, including the diaries of contemporaries and hundreds of affectionate and sometimes erotic letters written by James to younger men, the picture of neurotic celibacy gave way to a portrait of a closeted homosexual.

Between 1953 and 1972, Leon Edel authored a major five-volume biography of James, which accessed unpublished letters and documents after Edel gained the permission of James's family. Edel's portrayal of James included the suggestion he was celibate. It was a view first propounded by critic Saul Rosenzweig in 1943. In 1996 Sheldon M. Novick published Henry James: The Young Master, followed by Henry James: The Mature Master (2007). The first book "caused something of an uproar in Jamesian circles" as it challenged the previous received notion of celibacy, a once-familiar paradigm in biographies of homosexuals when direct evidence was non-existent. Novick also criticised Edel for following the discounted Freudian interpretation of homosexuality "as a kind of failure." The difference of opinion erupted in a series of exchanges between Edel and Novick which were published by the online magazine Slate, with the latter arguing that even the suggestion of celibacy went against James's own injunction "live!"—not "fantasize!"

A letter James wrote in old age to Hugh Walpole has been cited as an explicit statement of this. Walpole confessed to him of indulging in "high jinks", and James wrote a reply endorsing it: "We must know, as much as possible, in our beautiful art, yours & mine, what we are talking about — & the only way to know it is to have lived & loved & cursed & floundered & enjoyed & suffered — I don't think I regret a single 'excess' of my responsive youth".

The interpretation of James as living a less austere emotional life has been subsequently explored by other scholars. The often intense politics of Jamesian scholarship has also been the subject of studies. Author Colm Tóibín has said that Eve Kosofsky Sedgwick's Epistemology of the Closet made a landmark difference to Jamesian scholarship by arguing that he be read as a homosexual writer whose desire to keep his sexuality a secret shaped his layered style and dramatic artistry. According to Tóibín such a reading "removed James from the realm of dead white males who wrote about posh people. He became our contemporary."

James's letters to expatriate American sculptor Hendrik Christian Andersen have attracted particular attention. James met the 27-year-old Andersen in Rome in 1899, when James was 56, and wrote letters to Andersen that are intensely emotional: "I hold you, dearest boy, in my innermost love, & count on your feeling me—in every throb of your soul". In a letter of 6 May 1904, to his brother William, James referred to himself as "always your hopelessly celibate even though sexagenarian Henry". How accurate that description might have been is the subject of contention among James's biographers,   but the letters to Andersen were occasionally quasi-erotic: "I put, my dear boy, my arm around you, & feel the pulsation, thereby, as it were, of our excellent future & your admirable endowment." To his homosexual friend Howard Sturgis, James could write: "I repeat, almost to indiscretion, that I could live with you. Meanwhile I can only try to live without you."

His numerous letters to the many young gay men among his close male friends are more forthcoming. In a letter to Howard Sturgis, following a long visit, James refers jocularly to their "happy little congress of two" and in letters to Hugh Walpole he pursues convoluted jokes and puns about their relationship, referring to himself as an elephant who "paws you oh so benevolently" and winds about Walpole his "well meaning old trunk". His letters to Walter Berry printed by the Black Sun Press have long been celebrated for their lightly veiled eroticism.

He corresponded in almost equally extravagant language with his many female friends, writing, for example, to fellow novelist Lucy Clifford: "Dearest Lucy! What shall I say? when I love you so very, very much, and see you nine times for once that I see Others! Therefore I think that—if you want it made clear to the meanest intelligence—I love you more than I love Others." To his New York friend Mary Cadwalader Jones: "Dearest Mary Cadwalader. I yearn over you, but I yearn in vain; & your long silence really breaks my heart, mystifies, depresses, almost alarms me, to the point even of making me wonder if poor unconscious & doting old Célimare [Jones's pet name for James] has 'done' anything, in some dark somnambulism of the spirit, which has ... given you a bad moment, or a wrong impression, or a 'colourable pretext' ... However these things may be, he loves you as tenderly as ever;

nothing, to the end of time, will ever detach him from you, & he remembers those Eleventh St. matutinal intimes hours, those telephonic matinées, as the most romantic of his life ..." His long friendship with American novelist Constance Fenimore Woolson, in whose house he lived for a number of weeks in Italy in 1887, and his shock and grief over her suicide in 1894, are discussed in detail in Edel's biography and play a central role in a study by Lyndall Gordon. (Edel conjectured that Woolson was in love with James and killed herself in part because of his coldness, but Woolson's biographers have objected to Edel's account.)

Works

Style and themes

James is one of the major figures of trans-Atlantic literature. His works frequently juxtapose characters from the Old World (Europe), embodying a feudal civilisation that is beautiful, often corrupt, and alluring, and from the New World (United States), where people are often brash, open, and assertive and embody the virtues—freedom and a more highly evolved moral character—of the new American society. James explores this clash of personalities and cultures, in stories of personal relationships in which power is exercised well or badly. His protagonists were often young American women facing oppression or abuse, and as his secretary Theodora Bosanquet remarked in her monograph Henry James at Work:

> When he walked out of the refuge of his study and into the world and looked around him, he saw a place of torment, where creatures of prey perpetually thrust their claws into the quivering flesh of doomed, defenseless children of light ... His novels are a repeated exposure of this wickedness, a reiterated and passionate plea for the fullest freedom of development, unimperiled by reckless and barbarous stupidity.

Critics have jokingly described three phases in the development of James's prose: "James I, James II, and The Old Pretender." He wrote short stories and plays. Finally, in his third and last period he returned to the long, serialised novel. Beginning in the second period, but most noticeably in the third, he increasingly abandoned direct statement in favour of frequent double negatives, and complex descriptive imagery. Single paragraphs began to run for page after page, in which an initial noun would be succeeded by pronouns surrounded by clouds of adjectives and prepositional clauses, far from their original referents, and verbs would be deferred and then preceded by a series of adverbs. The overall effect could be a vivid evocation of a scene as perceived by a sensitive observer. It has been debated whether this change of style was engendered by James's shifting from writing to dictating to a typist, a change made during the composition of What Maisie Knew.

In its intense focus on the consciousness of his major characters, James's later work foreshadows extensive developments in 20th century fiction. Indeed, he might have influenced stream-of-consciousness writers such as Virginia Woolf, who not only read some of his novels but also wrote essays about them. Both contemporary and modern readers have found the late style difficult and unnecessary; his friend Edith Wharton, who admired him greatly, said that there were passages in his work that were all but incomprehensible. James was harshly portrayed by H. G. Wells as a hippopotamus laboriously attempting to pick up a pea that had got into a corner of its cage. The "late James" style was ably parodied by Max Beerbohm in "The Mote in the Middle Distance".

More important for his work overall may have been his position as an expatriate, and in other ways an outsider, living in Europe. While he came from middle-class and provincial beginnings (seen from the perspective of European polite society) he worked very hard to gain access to all levels of society, and the settings of his fiction range from working class to aristocratic, and often describe the efforts of middle-class Americans to make their way in European capitals. He confessed he got some of his best story ideas from gossip at the dinner table or at country house weekends. He worked for a living, however, and lacked the experiences of select schools, university, and army service, the common bonds of masculine society. He was furthermore a man whose tastes and interests were, according to the prevailing standards of Victorian era Anglo-American culture, rather feminine, and who was shadowed by the cloud of prejudice that then and later accompanied suspicions of his homosexuality. Edmund Wilson famously compared James's objectivity to Shakespeare's:

One would be in a position to appreciate James better if one compared him with the dramatists of the seventeenth century—Racine and Molière, whom he resembles in form as well as in point of view, and even Shakespeare, when allowances are made for the most extreme differences in subject and form. These poets are not, like Dickens and Hardy, writers of melodrama—either humorous or pessimistic, nor secretaries of society like Balzac, nor prophets like Tolstoy: they are occupied simply with the presentation of conflicts of moral character, which they do not concern themselves about softening or averting. They do not indict society for these situations: they regard them as universal and inevitable. They do not even blame God for allowing them: they accept them as the conditions of life.

It is also possible to see many of James's stories as psychological thought-experiments. In his preface to the New York edition of The American he describes the development of the story in his mind as exactly such: the "situation" of an American, "some robust but insidiously beguiled and betrayed, some cruelly wronged, compatriot..." with the focus of the story being on the response of this wronged man. The Portrait of a Lady may be an experiment to see what happens when an idealistic young woman suddenly becomes very rich. In many of his tales, characters seem to exemplify alternative futures and possibilities, as most markedly in "The Jolly Corner", in which the protagonist and a ghost-doppelganger live alternative American and European lives; and in others, like The Ambassadors, an older James seems fondly to regard his own younger self facing a crucial moment.

Major novels

The first period of James's fiction, usually considered to have culminated in The Portrait of a Lady, concentrated on the contrast between Europe and America. The style of these novels is generally straightforward and, though personally characteristic, well within the norms of 19th-century fiction. Roderick Hudson (1875) is a Künstlerroman that traces the development of the title character, an extremely talented sculptor. Although the book shows some signs of immaturity—this was James's first serious attempt at a full-length novel—it has attracted favourable comment due to the vivid realisation of the three major characters: Roderick Hudson, superbly gifted but unstable and unreliable; Rowland Mallet, Roderick's limited but much more mature friend and patron; and Christina Light, one of James's most enchanting and maddening femmes fatales. The pair of Hudson and Mallet has been seen as representing the two sides of James's own nature: the wildly imaginative artist and the brooding conscientious mentor.

In The Portrait of a Lady (1881) James concluded the first phase of his career with a novel that remains his most popular piece of long fiction. The story is of a spirited young American woman, Isabel Archer, who "affronts her destiny" and finds it overwhelming. She inherits a large amount of money and subsequently becomes the victim of Machiavellian scheming by two American expatriates. The narrative is set mainly in Europe, especially in England and Italy. Generally regarded as the masterpiece of his early phase, The Portrait of a Lady is described as a psychological novel, exploring the minds of his characters, and almost a work of social science, exploring the differences between Europeans and Americans, the old and the new worlds.

The second period of James's career, which extends from the publication of The Portrait of a Lady through the end of the nineteenth century, features less popular novels including The Princess Casamassima, published serially in The Atlantic Monthly in 1885–1886, and The Bostonians, published serially in The Century Magazine during the same period. This period also featured James's celebrated Gothic novella, The Turn of the Screw.

The third period of James's career reached its most significant achievement in three novels published just around the start of the 20th century: The Wings of the Dove (1902), The Ambassadors (1903), and The Golden Bowl (1904). Critic F. O. Matthiessen called this "trilogy" James's major phase, and these novels have certainly received intense critical study. It was the second-written of the books, The Wings of the Dove (1902) that was the first published because it attracted no serialization. This novel tells the story of Milly Theale, an American heiress stricken with a serious disease, and her impact on the people around her. Some of these people befriend Milly with honourable motives, while others are more self-interested. James stated in his autobiographical books that Milly was based on Minny Temple, his beloved cousin who died at an early age of tuberculosis. He said that he attempted in the novel to wrap her memory in the "beauty and dignity of art".

Shorter narratives

James was particularly interested in what he called the "beautiful and blest nouvelle", or the longer form of short narrative. Still, he produced a number of very short stories in which he achieved notable compression of sometimes complex subjects. The following narratives are representative of James's achievement in the shorter forms of fiction.

- "A Tragedy of Error" (1864), short story

- "The Story of a Year" (1865), short story

- A Passionate Pilgrim (1871), novella

- Madame de Mauves (1874), novella

- Daisy Miller (1878), novella

- The Aspern Papers (1888), novella

- The Lesson of the Master (1888), novella

- The Pupil (1891), short story

- "The Figure in the Carpet" (1896), short story

- The Beast in the Jungle (1903), novella

- An International Episode (1878)

- Picture and Text

- Four Meetings (1885)

- A London Life, and Other Tales (1889)

- The Spoils of Poynton (1896)

- Embarrassments (1896)

- The Two Magics: The Turn of the Screw, Covering End (1898)

- A Little Tour of France (1900)

- The Sacred Fount (1901)

- Views and Reviews (1908)

- The Wings of the Dove, Volume I (1902)

- The Wings of the Dove, Volume II (1909)

- The Finer Grain (1910)

- The Outcry (1911)

- Lady Barbarina: The Siege of London, An International Episode and Other Tales (1922)

- The Birthplace (1922)

Plays

At several points in his career James wrote plays, beginning with one-act plays written for periodicals in 1869 and 1871 and a dramatisation of his popular novella Daisy Miller in 1882. From 1890 to 1892, having received a bequest that freed him from magazine publication, he made a strenuous effort to succeed on the London stage, writing a half-dozen plays of which only one, a dramatisation of his novel The American, was produced. This play was performed for several years by a touring repertory company and had a respectable run in London, but did not earn very much money for James. His other plays written at this time were not produced.

In 1893, however, he responded to a request from actor-manager George Alexander for a serious play for the opening of his renovated St. James's Theatre, and wrote a long drama, Guy Domville, which Alexander produced. There was a noisy uproar on the opening night, 5 January 1895, with hissing from the gallery when James took his bow after the final curtain, and the author was upset. The play received moderately good reviews and had a modest run of four weeks before being taken off to make way for Oscar Wilde's The Importance of Being Earnest, which Alexander thought would have better prospects for the coming season.

After the stresses and disappointment of these efforts James insisted that he would write no more for the theatre, but within weeks had agreed to write a curtain-raiser for Ellen Terry. This became the one-act "Summersoft", which he later rewrote into a short story, "Covering End", and then expanded into a full-length play, The High Bid, which had a brief run in London in 1907, when James made another concerted effort to write for the stage. He wrote three new plays, two of which were in production when the death of Edward VII on 6 May 1910 plunged London into mourning and theatres closed. Discouraged by failing health and the stresses of theatrical work, James did not renew his efforts in the theatre, but recycled his plays as successful novels. The Outcry was a best-seller in the United States when it was published in 1911. During the years 1890–1893 when he was most engaged with the theatre, James wrote a good deal of theatrical criticism and assisted Elizabeth Robins and others in translating and producing Henrik Ibsen for the first time in London.

Leon Edel argued in his psychoanalytic biography that James was traumatised by the opening night uproar that greeted Guy Domville, and that it plunged him into a prolonged depression. The successful later novels, in Edel's view, were the result of a kind of self-analysis, expressed in fiction, which partly freed him from his fears. Other biographers and scholars have not accepted this account, however; the more common view being that of F.O. Matthiessen, who wrote: "Instead of being crushed by the collapse of his hopes [for the theatre]... he felt a resurgence of new energy."

Non-fiction

Beyond his fiction, James was one of the more important literary critics in the history of the novel. In his classic essay The Art of Fiction (1884), he argued against rigid prescriptions on the novelist's choice of subject and method of treatment. He maintained that the widest possible freedom in content and approach would help ensure narrative fiction's continued vitality.

James wrote many valuable critical articles on other novelists; typical is his book-length study of Nathaniel Hawthorne, which has been the subject of critical debate. Richard Brodhead has suggested that the study was emblematic of James's struggle with Hawthorne's influence, and constituted an effort to place the elder writer "at a disadvantage." Gordon Fraser, meanwhile, has suggested that the study was part of a more commercial effort by James to introduce himself to British readers as Hawthorne's natural successor.

When James assembled the New York Edition of his fiction in his final years, he wrote a series of prefaces that subjected his own work to searching, occasionally harsh criticism.

At 22 James wrote The Noble School of Fiction for The Nation's first issue in 1865. He would write, in all, over 200 essays and book, art, and theatre reviews for the magazine.

For most of his life James harboured ambitions for success as a playwright. He converted his novel The American into a play that enjoyed modest returns in the early 1890s. In all he wrote about a dozen plays, most of which went unproduced. His costume drama Guy Domville failed disastrously on its opening night in 1895. James then largely abandoned his efforts to conquer the stage and returned to his fiction. In his Notebooks he maintained that his theatrical experiment benefited his novels and tales by helping him dramatise his characters' thoughts and emotions. James produced a small but valuable amount of theatrical criticism, including perceptive appreciations of Henrik Ibsen.

With his wide-ranging artistic interests, James occasionally wrote on the visual arts. Perhaps his most valuable contribution was his favourable assessment of fellow expatriate John Singer Sargent, a painter whose critical status has improved markedly in recent decades. James also wrote sometimes charming, sometimes brooding articles about various places he visited and lived in. His most famous books of travel writing include Italian Hours (an example of the charming approach) and The American Scene (most definitely on the brooding side).

James was one of the great letter-writers of any era. More than ten thousand of his personal letters are extant, and over three thousand have been published in a large number of collections. A complete edition of James's letters began publication in 2006, edited by Pierre Walker and Greg Zacharias. As of 2014, eight volumes have been published, covering the period from 1855 to 1880. James's correspondents included celebrated contemporaries like Robert Louis Stevenson, Edith Wharton and Joseph Conrad, along with many others in his wide circle of friends and acquaintances. The letters range from the "mere twaddle of graciousness" to serious discussions of artistic, social and personal issues.

Very late in life James began a series of autobiographical works: A Small Boy and Others, Notes of a Son and Brother, and the unfinished The Middle Years. These books portray the development of a classic observer who was passionately interested in artistic creation but was somewhat reticent about participating fully in the life around him.

Reception

Criticism, biographies and fictional treatments

James's work has remained steadily popular with the limited audience of educated readers to whom he spoke during his lifetime, and has remained firmly in the canon, but, after his death, some American critics, such as Van Wyck Brooks, expressed hostility towards James for his long expatriation and eventual naturalisation as a British subject. Other critics such as E. M. Forster complained about what they saw as James's squeamishness in the treatment of sex and other possibly controversial material, or dismissed his late style as difficult and obscure, relying heavily on extremely long sentences and excessively latinate language. Similarly Oscar Wilde criticised him for writing "fiction as if it were a painful duty". Vernon Parrington, composing a canon of American literature, condemned James for having cut himself off from America. Jorge Luis Borges wrote about him, "Despite the scruples and delicate complexities of James, his work suffers from a major defect: the absence of life." And Virginia Woolf, writing to Lytton Strachey, asked, "Please tell me what you find in Henry James. ... we have his works here, and

I read, and I can't find anything but faintly tinged rose water, urbane and sleek, but vulgar and pale as Walter Lamb. Is there really any sense in it?" The novelist W. Somerset Maugham wrote, "He did not know the English as an Englishman instinctively knows them and so his English characters never to my mind quite ring true," and argued "The great novelists, even in seclusion, have lived life passionately. Henry James was content to observe it from a window." Maugham nevertheless wrote, "The fact remains that those last novels of his, notwithstanding their unreality, make all other novels, except the very best, unreadable." Colm Tóibín observed that James "never really wrote about the English very well. His English characters don't work for me."

Despite these criticisms, James is now valued for his psychological and moral realism, his masterful creation of character, his low-key but playful humour, and his assured command of the language. In his 1983 book, The Novels of Henry James, Edward Wagenknecht offers an assessment that echoes Theodora Bosanquet's:

> "To be completely great," Henry James wrote in an early review, "a work of art must lift up the heart," and his own novels do this to an outstanding degree ... More than sixty years after his death, the great novelist who sometimes professed to have no opinions stands foursquare in the great Christian humanistic and democratic tradition. The men and women who, at the height of World War II, raided the secondhand shops for his out-of-print books knew what they were about. For no writer ever raised a braver banner to which all who love freedom might adhere.

William Dean Howells saw James as a representative of a new realist school of literary art which broke with the English romantic tradition epitomised by the works of Charles Dickens and William Makepeace Thackeray. Howells wrote that realism found "its chief exemplar in Mr. James... A novelist he is not, after the old fashion, or after any fashion but his own." F.R. Leavis championed Henry James as a novelist of "established pre-eminence" in The Great Tradition (1948), asserting that The Portrait of a Lady and The Bostonians were "the two most brilliant novels in the language." James is now prized as a master of point of view who moved literary fiction forward by insisting in showing, not telling, his stories to the reader. (Source: Wikipedia)

NOTABLE WORKS

NOVELS

Watch and Ward (1871)

Roderick Hudson (1875)

The American (1877)

The Europeans (1878)

Confidence (1879)

Washington Square (1880)

The Portrait of a Lady (1881)

The Bostonians (1886)

The Princess Casamassima (1886)

The Reverberator (1888)

The Tragic Muse (1890)

The Other House (1896)

The Spoils of Poynton (1897)

What Maisie Knew (1897)

The Awkward Age (1899)

The Sacred Fount (1901)

The Wings of the Dove (1902)

The Ambassadors (1903)

The Golden Bowl (1904)

The Whole Family (collaborative novel with eleven other authors, 1908)

The Outcry (1911)

The Ivory Tower (unfinished, published posthumously 1917)

The Sense of the Past (unfinished, published posthumously 1917)

SHORT STORIES AND NOVELLAS

A Tragedy of Error (1864)

The Story of a Year (1865)

A Landscape Painter (1866)

A Day of Days (1866)

My Friend Bingham (1867)

Poor Richard (1867)

The Story of a Masterpiece (1868)

A Most Extraordinary Case (1868)

A Problem (1868)

De Grey: A Romance (1868)

Osborne's Revenge (1868)

The Romance of Certain Old Clothes (1868)

A Light Man (1869)

Gabrielle de Bergerac (1869)

Travelling Companions (1870)

A Passionate Pilgrim (1871)

At Isella (1871)

Master Eustace (1871)

Guest's Confession (1872)

The Madonna of the Future (1873)

The Sweetheart of M. Briseux (1873)

The Last of the Valerii (1874)

Madame de Mauves (1874)

Adina (1874)

Professor Fargo (1874)

Eugene Pickering (1874)

Benvolio (1875)

Crawford's Consistency (1876)

The Ghostly Rental (1876)

Four Meetings (1877)

Rose-Agathe (1878, as Théodolinde)

Daisy Miller (1878)

Longstaff's Marriage (1878)

An International Episode (1878)

The Pension Beaurepas (1879)

A Diary of a Man of Fifty (1879)

A Bundle of Letters (1879)

The Point of View (1882)

The Siege of London (1883)

Impressions of a Cousin (1883)

Lady Barberina (1884)

Pandora (1884)

The Author of Beltraffio (1884)

Georgina's Reasons (1884)

A New England Winter (1884)

The Path of Duty (1884)

Mrs. Temperly (1887)

Louisa Pallant (1888)

The Aspern Papers (1888)

The Liar (1888)

The Modern Warning (1888, originally published as The Two Countries)

A London Life (1888)

The Patagonia (1888)

The Lesson of the Master (1888)

The Solution (1888)

The Pupil (1891)

Brooksmith (1891)

The Marriages (1891)

The Chaperon (1891)

Sir Edmund Orme (1891)

Nona Vincent (1892)

The Real Thing (1892)

The Private Life (1892)

Lord Beaupré (1892)

The Visits (1892)

Sir Dominick Ferrand (1892)

Greville Fane (1892)

Collaboration (1892)

Owen Wingrave (1892)

The Wheel of Time (1892)

The Middle Years (1893)

The Death of the Lion (1894)

The Coxon Fund (1894)

The Next Time (1895)

Glasses (1896)

The Altar of the Dead (1895)

The Figure in the Carpet (1896)

The Way It Came (1896, also published as The Friends of the Friends)

The Turn of the Screw (1898)

Covering End (1898)

In the Cage (1898)

John Delavoy (1898)

The Given Case (1898)

Europe (1899)

The Great Condition (1899)

The Real Right Thing (1899)

Paste (1899)

The Great Good Place (1900)

Maud-Evelyn (1900)

Miss Gunton of Poughkeepsie (1900)

The Tree of Knowledge (1900)

The Abasement of the Northmores (1900)

The Third Person (1900)

The Special Type (1900)

The Tone of Time (1900)

Broken Wings (1900)

The Two Faces (1900)

Mrs. Medwin (1901)

The Beldonald Holbein (1901)

The Story in It (1902)

Flickerbridge (1902)

The Birthplace (1903)

The Beast in the Jungle (1903)

The Papers (1903)

Fordham Castle (1904)

Julia Bride (1908)

The Jolly Corner (1908)

The Velvet Glove (1909)

Mora Montravers (1909)

Crapy Cornelia (1909)

The Bench of Desolation (1909)

A Round of Visits (1910)

OTHER

Transatlantic Sketches (1875)

French Poets and Novelists (1878)

Hawthorne (1879)

Portraits of Places (1883)

A Little Tour in France (1884)

Partial Portraits (1888)

Essays in London and Elsewhere (1893)

Picture and Text (1893)

Terminations (1893)

Theatricals (1894)

Theatricals: Second Series (1895)

Guy Domville (1895)

The Soft Side (1900)

William Wetmore Story and His Friends (1903)

The Better Sort (1903)

English Hours (1905)

The Question of our Speech; The Lesson of Balzac. Two Lectures (1905)

The American Scene (1907)

Views and Reviews (1908)

Italian Hours (1909)

A Small Boy and Others (1913)

Notes on Novelists (1914)

Notes of a Son and Brother (1914)

Within the Rim (1918)

Travelling Companions (1919)

Notebooks (various, published posthumously)

The Middle Years (unfinished, published posthumously 1917)

A Most Unholy Trade (1925, published posthumously)

The Art of the Novel : Critical Prefaces (1934)

CPSIA information can be obtained
at www.ICGtesting.com
Printed in the USA
LVHW040133031120
670492LV00021B/747